Death at Versailles

a&b

Death at Versailles

JANE JAKEMAN

First published in Great Britain in 2002 by
Allison & Busby Limited
Bon Marche Centre
241-251 Ferndale Road
Brixton, London SW9 8BJ
http://www.allisonandbusby.com

This is a work of fiction and all characters, firms, organisations and instants portrayed are imaginary. They are not meant to resemble any counterparts in the real world; in the unlikely event that any similarity does exist it is an unintended coincidence.

A catalogue record for this book is available from the British Library

ISBN 0 7490 0589 0

Printed and bound in Ebbw Vale,
by Creative Print & Design

JANE JAKEMAN is an author, freelance journalist and art historian whose previous trilogy of historical crime novels featured Byronic detective, Lord Ambrose Malfine. Born in Wales, she has travelled widely and is a great lover of French culture. She regularly reviews crime fiction for the *Independent*. *Death at Versailles* is the second in the series featuring examining magistrate, Cecile Galant.

For JM as always and
with grateful thanks to Michèle Riley

Chapter One

'Take care!' said Luke, anxiously.

Why was he fussing so? Marina was tense for no reason, almost began to feel impatient, looking out of the café window at the small groups of waiting travellers, their luggage stashed awkwardly at their knees as they watched the announcement screens. Then, as his dark blue eyes looked down seriously at her face, she also felt guilty.

Because Luke cared about her. And if she wanted to get away, why, she knew the reason for that, and it had nothing to do with poor Luke, and everything to do with Marina herself, who was desperate to leave, as she now admitted silently.

'I'll get you a coffee,' said Luke.

Tightening her fingers round the coffee cup in the little Costa Coffee bar, then tracing lines absent-mindedly in the spilt khaki froth on the table-top, Marina made herself face the truth. 'It's a form of running away,' she told herself. 'To where, no one knows ...'

'Sorry?' she said aloud, aware that he had just said something in a really serious tone, yet unable to think what it could have been, her own thoughts blotting out his voice.

Damn, the more she did that, the worse he thought her. He seemed to be made a bit cross anyway by her lapse of attention, but put out his hand and clasped her wet fingers protectively.

'I said, "You will ring me the minute you feel there's anything wrong?"'

'Yes, of course,' she said, 'Of course, I will.' He seemed satisfied, leaning back a little, his face pale and the lines tight around his mouth, but less intense.

But what she really wanted to do was just to go. To France, to Paris, to any place where they didn't know about her.

As she felt sometimes everybody did, not just in Woodstock, but when she went into college, even walking round Oxford. As though people were murmuring, 'yes, that's her, that's the one who ...'

Sometimes she looked at her dark reflection in shop windows and wondered about herself. 'That's the one!'

Outside the café they could hear the announcer calling passengers to board the train. She scrutinised her ticket anxiously, checked her seat number, stood up and collected her coat. Luke took the little case from her as they walked towards the Eurostar entrance. 'Sure you've got enough in here?'

'Oh, yes, I'll only need a few things. I'm just going for a week, after all. See you very soon, then!'

She managed a smile, and as he bent down and kissed her, putting his arms tightly round her, she wondered why she could have felt so disloyal to him.

'All right, but ring me when you get there. And Marina ...'

'Yes?'

'I shouldn't say - well, I shouldn't say anything to anybody about it. About what happened. You know what I mean?'

'Who on earth would I tell? I'm not going to see anyone I know - it's just research, after all.'

He relaxed, and smiled at her, the great big grin that she had first noticed and liked about him, the thing she had always loved.

'There aren't many people lucky enough to get to Versailles for a research trip. Enjoy it, darling, don't work too hard!'

Things were settling into normality again.

She took the handle of the case and went through the barrier, turning to wave at him. His tall figure was obscured as other passengers crowded after her and she felt a moment's panic: could she really manage on her own, after what had happened?

But she moved through the terminal to the gate and up the ramp, and when she saw the great gleaming train standing at the platform, in spite of herself, she felt an enormous sensation of relief. To get away, that was it. That was she wanted, underneath, deep down, to show the world she was capable of running her own life again.

Chapter Two

'*Chérie*, it's time to go!'

Violetta, calling from the bedroom, answered him with a question.

'Do you want me to drive you to the station?'

'Yes, I thought you said you would.'

Chief Inspector Pierre Maubourg looked into the shaving mirror to give a final check, noting the deep hound-dog folds, the weary eyelids. 'I look like a parody of a French cop,' he thought to himself, and the hound-dog disappeared into a grin.

Violetta appeared in the bedroom doorway, in some dark green dress that made her look as slim as a reed. She was perched elegantly on top of a pair of lizardskin shoes with precipitous heels, simultaneously pulling on a jacket and reaching for her car-keys, which had been tossed into their usual location in a blue china bowl on the hall shelf. 'Damn, I'll have to change my shoes. I think I left my flat heels in the car. No, Pierre, I don't remember you saying anything about it, but I suppose if you're ready now I can take you. Aren't they sending an official car for you?'

'No, this isn't an official trip.'

He heard his voice, thought he sounded a bit irritable with her.

'Where are you going, then?'

He hesitated. There could really be no danger in her knowing.

'To Versailles. I have to see someone there.'

She twirled suddenly on a precarious spike, and made a mock curtsey.

'Versailles! Well, we are going up in the world, but there's only one person you know there! Madame the judge, isn't it? Well, well, have you two got something going between you?'

She was laughing, but the usual edginess between them could come back at any moment, he knew.

'Where are you going, Papa?'

Their teenage daughter, Rachelle, emerged from her room and before he could say anything Violetta answered, 'Your father's going to Versailles, darling. Imagine, he's shooting into high society!'

'Really, Papa? We're doing the Revolution at school.'

Rachelle had inherited Maubourg's brown eyes, rather than her mother's exquisite great blue-violet spell-binders, and his solid jaw also, but she was bidding, unexpectedly, to develop the same delicate leggy grace as Violetta. Now she moved, long-limbed, her feet stuck into sneakers, into the hall of their apartment, which seemed already to be starting to heat up for the August day in Cannes. Soon the crowds would be surging on the esplanades and the beaches, the scarlet lilies in the flowerbeds along the Croisette would be wilting, the Casino touts would be fastening their cuff-links and strutting the pavements.

Maubourg wanted to get away, but he needed to say something to Rachelle.

'Darling, don't say anything at school.'

'What do you mean?'

'About my visit to Versailles, I mean. Don't tell anyone I've gone there.'

'Why, is it about something dangerous?'

Rachelle's eyes were suddenly big with excitement. She was just beginning to realise that her father was sometimes mixed up in events that could be perilous, things that she had to keep quiet about. Yet in spite of her excitement he trusted her not to talk about his police work. It was just that, like most people, she probably associated a visit to Versailles with French history, with tourism, and might not think it was to do with his work. He had a feeling of security in telling things to Rachelle, though he had always tried to shield her from the truth of his work, the cruelties and violence of it. Not all on the side of the criminals, he had to admit. There were some prejudices and brutalities inherent on his side of the fence, also, it had to be admitted. But on the whole, he thought, she hadn't been given too many nightmares when her father came home from work, though it had been pretty terrible during the investigation of the 'Cannes Mutilator', when the details of the torn and grotesque corpses of the victims had been splashed across the news-stands.

'No, it's not dangerous at all - but it's better if people don't know about it. Just don't say anything, Rachelle - that's all.'

'All right, I promise. But only if you tell me all about it when you get home!'

'How will you know?' Violetta teased her. 'How will you know if he's told you the truth?'

'How indeed?' he thought to himself. 'And how do I know, Violetta, my wife, Rachelle's mother, how do I know if you've got a lover now? That's one more thing we're not going to talk about, besides the Versailles trip.'

But these thoughts passed swiftly in his mind and he put his arms round his daughter.

'That's fine, darling. See you in a day or two.'

Like Rachelle, Violetta was used to secrets in their lives. She knew there were things in a policeman's life that his family could not know, questions they shouldn't ask. Did he trust her about that? He didn't know any more, that was the honest truth. How can you trust a person in one compartment of your mind and not another? Trust her to keep your professional secrets and yet not to be faithful?

They were getting into Violetta's little VW, pulling out in the direction of the station and the long fast journey to Paris in the TGV.

'Have you booked?'

'Yes. Only to Paris.'

He wanted to go, now, to get out of the tourist hubbub that would envelop his town, to go now while his wife was still smiling and affectionate. As the car slowed and came to a halt, he gave her a swift kiss on the cheek and flung himself out into the station forecourt. 'I'll ring you when I get there. If anyone asks where I've got to, just tell them I've had to go to Paris. Administration, something like that.'

'I'll be the soul of discretion. But when you come back you'll have to tell me all about little Madame Galant!'

She laughed and the car tore off with a shriek of the tyres towards the travel agency where she worked.

Violetta would be happier as a conspirator than as a wife, he thought, remembering *Liaisons Dangereuses*. Perhaps some people just had that temperament naturally, the taste for intrigue, the talent for it. Maybe they didn't even need to actually indulge.

Anyway, he trusted her about Versailles, and with this thought he boarded the train.

Chapter Three

Élise looked out of the window at the deserted street. She felt restless, not wanting to light another cigarette. It looked too cold to go out, the usual lunchtime crowd wouldn't yet be in the café, but she was bored with staying in and had welcomed Marie's phone-call.

'Are you going to be in this morning? Yes, I can come round - want to talk to you, anyway.'

She missed her friend Marie's frequent visits, but there it was - Toni did not like Marie to call round as she always used to do, and somehow Marie had ended up doing what he told her. Now she hardly ever came to see Élise - once every few weeks, maybe.

'I'd give him what for,' said Élise to herself, and yet a flicker of fear ran through her at the thought of his face, the expression she had seen on it when they had encountered a petty thief who might have tried to pick Toni's wallet in a bar where they had stopped for drinks. As he twisted on his bar-stool, Toni's eyes had a kind of savagery that made the punk slide out of the door and they could hear his footsteps running down the street, pounding away as fast as he could go.

Not that she had ever had cause to think that Toni treated Marie badly - she had never had a black eye or anything serious. But it was just - well, what was it, exactly? That he gave all the orders? Not really, though he did tell Marie what to do a lot of the time. But it was more things he didn't say, looking at her in such a suspicious sort of way.

But this was a day when Marie had got out, and there she was, hurrying down the street. She took off her coat and Élise saw she was wearing her blue dress with white flowers on it, the one that was quite sexy, off one shoulder, that she had bought with Élise when they went shopping together last month.

'He doesn't want me to come any more,' Marie said, running a hand through her hair, when they were curled up with cups of coffee.

Élise lit a cigarette and flicked towards an ashtray.

'But we don't do anything, nothing he could complain about, anyway - just go out for a drink sometimes!'

Well, that was understating it, perhaps - but after all, there was no real harm in Marie.

'That's not the point, really. Not for him, anyway. He likes to go out to that place in the country he told me about. I think he wants me to go there too.'

'But you wouldn't want that, surely? Why don't you tell him to get stuffed?'

There was a long pause. 'She's scared of him,' thought Élise. But it was more than that.

'I'm pregnant.'

'Oh, God! Why don't you do something about it?'

'I don't know if I want to go through with it, that's true.'

Marie fiddled with the buckle on her bag.

'You're surely not going to have it - a kid by him?'

But her friend only looked up unhappily. Her face looked thinner; perhaps it was being pregnant. It didn't suit some women.

Élise said, 'Well then, make it your decision.'

But she knew somehow, without their having to talk about it, just deep down within her, that Marie wouldn't, couldn't, do that, she wasn't going to make up her mind to have an abortion, all on her own. She was too much in bondage to the bloody man.

'Surely you can call round sometimes, just here? He can't object to that. And how would he know about it?'

'Yes, I suppose I could - if we went to a bar, he'd find out somehow - one of his pals would see us, or something.'

'Well, then.'

Élise was impatient with her friend, but she looked affectionately at her, the long hair that seemed damp with perspiration. Marie was hollow-eyed, as if she wasn't sleeping. Still, perhaps it would make her happy enough, to have the kid, even if Toni fucked off, because that was what would surely happen. Élise couldn't see that one being tied down by a kid, though Marie might manage on her own. But then Élise was startled by something Marie said.

'If you didn't see me for a while - would you ... would you try to find me?'

Élise was taken aback, but she quickly said, 'Of course, I would, *ma petite chérie*. But what is it - why don't you go to the police? Are you really afraid *he* would do something?'

There was no need to say the name.

'Oh, no, of course not!' Marie gave a laugh, but it didn't sound right.

'No, I just have silly fantasies sometimes. And it occurred to me, it's the test of a true friend - would they go looking for you, if you disappeared? How many people like that do you know? That's a definition of friendship, don't you think? And here in Versailles, this snobby place with all these important people - somehow, I feel as if people like us don't count - you know, that no one would notice if something happened -'

Marie broke off.

Too proud to admit it, Élise thought. Too proud to admit that Toni would be a disaster as a husband - and Marie's own family hate him. They wouldn't ever come out from Paris to see Marie - not that Toni would welcome it if they did.

Not for the first time, she said, 'Why don't you leave him? Just walk out.'

But she knew the answer to that - you didn't just walk out on men like Toni. To a man like that, a woman who didn't want him committed an act of deadly insult which would never be overlooked: where sex was concerned, such men thought only in terms of humiliation to themselves and punishment to others.

'You don't know him like I do!' said Marie. 'He can be wonderful sometimes, you know.'

'And I am the Queen of Romania!'

All the same, Élise wondered if she was getting too worked up about it. It was Marie's business, after all, and she knew the bloody man a lot better than Élise did.

'Don't take any notice of me,' Marie was saying now. 'I've just been a bit depressed, that's all. Forget it.'

Élise did. Almost.

Chapter Four

The afternoon had an odd, still quality, which was a welcome relief.

It had probably been a mistake to come in August, though she hadn't told Luke so, just that she had arrived safely, no, she had no problems, all was well, the Auberge du Duc perfectly comfortable.

The atmosphere clung hot and heavy, and there was no breeze. But she had really come to France at that time of year to escape, if the truth be known, from more than a dreadful remembrance. Marina thought Oxford in August was an inner circle of hell itself, its cramped streets given over to teenagers and tourists, the warm damp Thames valley air descending like cottonwool on dirty streets and thirsty dogs.

The great cobbled courtyard of the Château of Versailles held knots of tourists speaking every language under the sun, but there was not too much of a queue for the entrance to the State Apartments, and Marina was soon drifting through the great and dazzling salons. At times, her eyes seemed to be almost blinded from all the glitter. So much gold - suns and stars and gilt chairs and winking brass hinges, tortoiseshell and gold leaf, red and gold silk, all flashing in the light and glimmering again in the depths of mirrors. After an hour or so, she longed for some dimness, for a little cool neglect and greyish-silver tarnishing. Speaking to Luke on the phone that morning had almost made her homesick for misty Oxfordshire, but she was thinking of its perfections in the spring, not its heavy summer days.

The Hall of Mirrors stretched away in a dream-like sequence of dim windows giving on to landscapes of the past, and the never-ending stream of tourists floated through it. The great chandeliers hung in space like silvery comets, their bodies fiery with touches of gold. Satiny gleams and ripples in the marble panels, white folds in dark-green or pewter-grey surfaces, reflected the light like rocks glimpsed beneath overhanging cascades, as if polished by the incessant flow of luminescent waterfalls. How many windows were there? Seventeen, she counted, and the very number, indivisible, inexplicable, was somehow disorienting and added to the dream-like sensations. Seventeen huge arched windows, and opposite each a great arched mirror, its counterpart, taking and giving back the light of day.

Marina wanted to concentrate better as she gazed up at Le Brun's famous painted ceiling, trying to decipher the figures, rioting in cloaks and bits of Roman armour, who emerged from clouds and gestured imperiously through the stratosphere. 'Glorious episodes from the Dutch War', said her guide-book and she faithfully tried to understand some of the events depicted. As she stared upwards at a scene of conquest, the painted figures seemed to be plunging, flying through space and, turning round on the spot to try and follow them, she seemed almost to lose the sense of solid ground beneath her feet. High above her head, a chariot hurtled over a group of cowering figures who fell beneath its wheels. The conquered men were half-clad, their bare outstretched arms and shoulders with great rippling muscles outlined beneath their dark skin. A woman fell back in the wake of the chariot, her garment falling from one shoulder to reveal a shining white naked breast. Grotesque figures, their hair flowing, followed the rearing horses.

What wildness, thought Marina, what frenzy, framed in such a pretty gilded treasure-box. I never realised this.

She moved aside for a party of Japanese tourists, bringing her gaze down to earth for a few moments. Some of the Japanese trotted blindly with short cautious steps, not bothering to take their eyes from the video-cameras through which they viewed and modified this extraordinary world.

When they had passed, she moved on a few paces, and peered down at her guide-book, her eyes re-focusing on the print. She should be under the great central composition, 'The Young King turning away from Pleasure and Sports to contemplate the Crown of Immortality offered to him by Glory.'

Marina looked up once more, turning her head. High above her, in the midst of a feast of umber and gold, within hues of scarlet and bronze and the creamy glistening tones of ermine, a woman reached out towards the figure of Louis XIV, the Sun-King, absolute monarch of all he surveyed. Her magnificent plump body, smooth-skinned, narrow-waisted, with an opulent soft belly, was naked down to the hips and her flesh gleamed beside the white fur of his robe. Tiny naked cherubs surrounded the throne, playing at cards and chequers. The lush, silky, physicality of pleasure, disarrayed and casually, almost violently, enjoyed, unfolded on high. And across the centre of the ceiling, seeming to tumble through space, flew a giddy, disorienting and plunging Mercury.

As she followed his winged and glittering trajectory through the painted clouds above her head, dizziness overcame Marina. 'I'll have to come back another time,' she thought, as we so often do when we are overwhelmed by some great work of art. 'It's too much to take in all at once.'

She stopped craning her neck, and the dizzy feeling left her as she moved on, her imagination working. There would have been white damask curtains and silver furniture with crystal ornaments, the chandeliers and candelabra blazing forth. The gallery would have been thronged with courtiers as the King moved through in brilliant procession, petitions thrust at him as he passed.

But the thoughts that normally stimulated her fascination with the past seemed merely on this occasion to exhaust her. She reached a staircase with relief, and descended to ground level. Hadn't she read somewhere of the less attractive habits of the courtiers - that they relieved themselves under the stairs?

It was an unpleasant thought, and Marina wandered out into the gardens.

Chapter Five

Marina was walking without thinking or planning, simply wanting to rest her eyes on the green lawns and feel the cooler air around the sprays and cascades that were playing at the end of the long walk. She knew there was a little electric train that ran through the grounds, from the main building to the two Trianons, the small palaces that the Kings and Queens of France had built for their amusement, but she wanted a walk in the air.

Her head felt heavy: the scar was aching now. It had probably been a mistake to stay so late in the afternoon: still, there were fewer tourists round at this time of day. Most of them had long been safely on the road back to Paris and were now in the comfort of their hotels, their throbbing feet raised blissfully on couches. She thought of being home in England with Luke, of cool fields, the happier memories. She took her shoes off and walked on the grass for a while, its silky fronds brushing her bare feet. The gleaming sheet of water seemed endless; the trees rose on the other side of the lake in graceful interlacing arches as if covering some huge natural ballroom half-familiar from paintings by Watteau, where fragile creatures danced, embarked, and loved.

Further and further she moved down beside the long walk, away from the thinning armies of crowds, past a few hardy tourist outposts, mostly taking photographs of the Château. Versailles was spread out like a perfect tapestry, each strand, every square plotted and knotted into place. There was hardly anyone about at the end of the long promenade, beside the great fountain, just a couple of Americans, plump middle-aged women wearing sneakers with their bags slung round their middles in that curious defensive way. They had ventured further than the rest of their group and were evidently worried about getting back. They looked at their watches as she passed and one of them was saying 'Four-thirty? It's that already!'

The grounds were dotted with classical statues, spouting fountains, nymphs with falling drapery, bearded male gods and cavorting infants. Marina didn't really pause to look at them. She turned off to her right and walked along a path that led away from the main walk, emerging into several small open spaces occupied by fountains. One of them was being drained and the muddy smell rose unpleasantly into the August air: a dank rim of scum indicated where the level of the water had been lowered. In the middle, an improbably powerful-looking naked figure covered with rich dark red-gold leaf held a conch to his lips: Neptune, perhaps, or some lesser marine deity.

Looking down into the basin of the fountain, she saw a fluttering movement. There was a fish struggling in the few inches of mud at the bottom: the scaly back was an arched bow, sticking up above the level of the small remaining patch of moisture. The thing tried to burrow deeper, then flipped and jumped in desperation, gasping, only to fall back into the ooze. It would die soon. Marina thought that some provision must have been made to remove the fish before the drainage was undertaken, but this lone survivor had escaped the nets.

She could do something about it, she supposed. There was no one else within sight, and the fish, which looked like some sort of carp or giant goldfish, would die long before anyone else, some official who could rescue it, came along. She might go back to the Château and tell someone, but it was a long way, and would they take any notice?

She found she could not bear to look at the dying leaps and twitches and turned her head, beginning to walk away, but she could still hear the splattering sounds as the creature crashed down into the mud.

Sighing, she remembered something, and pulled a thin scarf out of her pocket. It was a red and white chiffon one, not expensive, but she was fond of it. She went back to the fountain, hoping that the fish would have died in the few seconds it had taken her to make her decision. But it still jerked feebly, though weaker now, unable to leap above the mud. The sun was beating down and the mud had dried into crusts at the edges: soon it would be caked hard.

Marina looked round again. There didn't seem to be anybody in sight. Feeling silly, quixotic, irredeemably foolish, she rolled up her jeans, pulled off her shoes and stepped into the fountain.

The mud was surprisingly pleasant to the feet, cool, squelching up between her toes. Tying three corners of her scarf together, she formed it into a kind of bag, and managed to drag it underneath the fish. The fountain stank as she bent her head down to the mud.

She lifted her makeshift fish-net, pulling the scarf tighter to stop the creature from wriggling out. 'Stupid thing!' she thought. 'Why can't it be still?'

And then it did seem to go quite still and she thought it was dead, but by this time she had advanced along the path, mud dripping from her burden. There was a tank that seemed to be some kind of feeder a few yards to one side, and she untangled her scarf and dropped the fish in. Peering down, thinking it would float to the surface belly-up, she was surprised to see it flipping in the water, and after an instant it arched its back again and then dived to the bottom, and she could see nothing more except a faint string of bubbles.

The scarf was filthy and smelling, but she managed to rinse off the worst of it, and washed her feet, too. No one had followed her along this side path, or witnessed her peculiar behaviour. The water in the tank seemed relatively clean and deep. She sat on the warm grass for a little while, and gradually everything seemed to dry off.

Marina realised that she had walked a long way now, mostly down straight paths lined with trees. She got up, her shoes in her hand, and moved on, the avenues of possibilities opening geometrically in front of her, but she knew her general direction, had studied it carefully on the map in advance. She was relieved, nevertheless, to see the small building, quite close, far out of sight of the Château. There was a sprinkling of visitors, now, on one of the paths, but they passed along, a gently-browsing herd moving across the great tourist Serengeti of Versailles. Marina made her way slowly towards her goal. It was ornate and careful, solid stone, like a minor version of a Château, a four-square building of classical proportions.

Anywhere but in these grounds it could almost pass for a mansion: here it was dwarfed by the scale of its surroundings.

There was a courtyard with a long perron at one side. She paused on the steps and put her shoes back on, with a vague sense of ... was it of being back in civilisation? Or was it that she was being watched?

This had to be the place, the Petit Trianon: she recognised it from photographs in the guide-books.

'I know the gardens, too,' she murmured. The formal French garden must be to the left, and the 'English garden', an area of 'natural' landscaping, to the right. Moving around the house, she came out behind it and crossed some velvety lawns studded with clumps of trees. Then came a stream which ran into a pool fringed with ornamental rocks and ferns, and a path leading up around a little contrived wooden knoll. Perched on the slope was a pretty circular building, like a small Greek temple, with miniature stone sphinxes around a low outer wall. That was known as the Belvedere.

The whole area reminded her of the grounds of some great English mansion, but on a tiny scale. That stream - in reality one could cross it with three or four paces. The rustic wooden bridge was slender and flimsy, the steep 'hillside' was no more than twenty feet high, yet how skilfully the eye was deceived into thinking this a larger landscape.

Just so, those two women must have been deceived.

It must have been just here. Yes, about here, at any rate, that it had happened.

Her mouth was dry, and she decided to stop in a minute, have a drink from her bottle of mineral water, and look at the map in her guide-book to see exactly where she was.

Now there was no one about and all sounds had died behind her. Her footsteps made no sound, cushioned in her thick-soled shoes. Silence, grass, heat.

Climbing up towards the temple-style building, she suddenly saw two things. Something white, familiar in general shape, jerky in its movement, and another thing or person, something darker. Closer, closer, she walked.

Her heart pounded when she couldn't make sense of things. These moments sometimes came now, fearful seconds that had to be driven away with action. She found she was walking faster.

At first it was quite normal. Just another tourist, a man dressed in white, and suddenly part of her vision resolved itself into another figure, a thin smaller one, with his hair dressed back in a long 'queue', emerging from the shadows of the building. The two figures merged, with the smaller one in front of the other, outside the little temple. And then there was a scream, a thin desperate sound that echoed through the hot August air and was quickly silenced: she saw a white-clad arm reach up and flash across a face, and the screaming stopped. There was a curious, jerking movement, legs kicking, a head snapping back.

The darker figure fell into the grass.

The first shape disappeared round the side of the building.

Marina could not believe it. The whole day had been spent amid the extravagant fantasy of Versailles, its mad and absurd conjurations of the past, and now, in the twenty-first century, here was something beyond any credulity.

But there was no doubt. The man in white had raced away behind the building, and there was a guttural bubbling sound coming from the grass, where she saw, a moment or two later, the face of a boy. His neck was at a dreadful angle.

But it was his hair and clothing that was so strange.

His mouth opened in a spasm and through her mind flitted a ridiculous idea of giving him some water. She had no control over the bitter vomit that rushed into her throat at the thought, managing to turn her face aside so that she didn't splash the poor dying thing.

Chapter Six

They were waiting in a car in the courtyard, which was full of activity.

One of the policemen was talking into a phone, the other, his arm extending in directions from time to time, was giving instructions to an official who was standing at the top of the steps. Tourists had been allowed to file back on to their coaches, but they were not allowed to leave. They sat obediently, in their phalanxes, grouped by nation, their guides and interpreters bobbing up and down in the aisles.

An black unmarked van drew up and swirled around the great courtyard of the Château, where once, at night, a carriage had been espied taking away the body of the Pompadour, the breasts outlined beneath a sheet. Marina remembered reading the description.

The policeman at the top of the steps, neat in a short-sleeved white shirt, came down to the car and got in the back, next to her.

'We have sent for an interpreter.'

His English was good, anyway. 'You will have to make a statement to us at the police station.'

Marina nodded. She felt extremely cold in spite of the heat and the man looked at her with a kind of professional assessment, got out of the car and walked to the boot, drawing out a blanket.

'You are in shock.'

Then he leaned forward and was talking rapid French to the driver. She could follow it, so her brain must still be functioning. But she was in shock, he was right.

Yes, she knew it as she pulled the blanket round her, knew what it felt like, the dazed mind, the inner core of icy cold that nothing seemed to reach. She felt anxiously for her bag, suddenly worried about her possessions, seizing with relief onto the thick leather strap. Where was her passport? In the hotel, surely. She remembered thinking it would be safest there, at the reception.

She had lost all sense of time, but looking at her watch she saw that an unbelievably short space had passed, perhaps twenty minutes, at most. It had seemed to take forever, running back towards the Château, gasping at a frightened-looking group of people who didn't seem to have a word of English. At last she had seen an Italian boy talking into his mobile and she ran to him, saying over and over, 'police, call the police,' till at last he cut off his call and began pressing buttons. Alarms began to sound all over the place and in a few minutes a uniformed attendant, attracted by the commotion, was coming from the direction of the Grand Trianon and she had pulled him along, gasping because she had never seemed to catch her breath, towards the Château and safety.

As they got closer, with heavy stumbling steps that were like the dragging leaden running in a nightmare, she was afraid it would no longer be there, that there would be nothing solid left, as in a nightmare where everything one can cling onto dissolves like mist. But suddenly there was the great structure of the Château, the most fantastic mansion in history, yet real and solid, and people were running out of the building towards her. The landscape was empty: the skies still blue as ever. The whole episode seemed to have struck at her by some dreadful mistake: something that really should have happened to someone else, somewhere else.

Huddled now in the blanket in the back of the police car, she closed her eyes and squeezed her lids tight shut, rubbing them with the back of her hand. She ran her fingers through her short hair, feeling the thin raised ridge of scalp.

Damn. She wished she hadn't done that. The policeman was looking at her. The hair was sparse on that side. He must have seen the scar.

Chapter Seven

The woman who came in with a rush and a rapid greeting was thin, with short fair hair and a dark suit. They lined up in the small office, Marina, the young interpreter, another official-looking man who had a notebook ready. The woman sat on the other side of the big desk, waving them all to the chairs in front of her. Her face was high-cheekboned and elegant, but somehow she did not have the look of a vain woman.

There was no question of who was in charge, but she made a formal pronouncement.

'I am Cecile Galant, the *juge d'instruction* in charge of this investigation. My job is to conduct an impartial investigation into the facts of a crime.'

She had remarkable eyes, very direct. She looked straight at Marina's face, a quick, piercing glance, then turned to some papers on the desk.

The interpreter rendered what she had said into English, adding an explanation. 'The *juge d'instruction,* that is what you would call an examining magistrate, or an instructing judge ...'

Marina interrupted in French. 'It's all right, madame, I don't need the interpreter.'

'You are sure?'

'My mother was French. I'm bilingual.'

'Very good.' The woman nodded towards the interpreter. 'You may leave.' She turned towards the other man present. 'This person taking notes is what we call a *greffier* - that is, he is my clerk.'

She told the interpreter he could leave. When he went out, Marina wondered if she had been right, even though the young man looked as if he had just graduated from college. Language is a state of mind, as well as words, she thought. But she had committed herself.

'Mademoiselle, you claim to have witnessed - what, exactly?'

'Claim,' thought Marina. 'Why "claim?" I saw it.'

She said aloud, 'I saw someone having ... his neck broken.'

The pause was not so much because she had to search for the French words but because in the split-second before she was going to utter it, she realised how shocking it was.

The throat held in a death-grip, the life snapped out.

But there was no reaction of horror on the other side of the desk. 'This woman is cold,' Marina thought to herself, 'but maybe she's seen a lot.'

Mme Galant's voice came very quietly, as if deliberately injecting calm into the proceedings.

'Please tell me exactly what you saw. My clerk is recording what you say.'

The official-looking man had moved to a typewriter, rather old-fashioned looking, and his hands were poised over the keys, which formed a rapid intermittent clacking accompaniment to Marina's words. Sounds seemed to echo in this room.

They went through much of the information that Marina had already given to the police inspector, the first account she had given of something, she realised, that would now become ritualised, repeated, set in stone.

'And there was this extraordinary business of the clothes ...'

'Yes - well, your policemen must have seen - I suppose there was some party, or maybe a fête of some sort ...'

'Please describe them for me.'

The voice was quite sharp, almost reprimanding.

Marina stared for a moment. Then she began again.

'The clothes. Well, yes it was peculiar - but, given the circumstances -'

She told the woman again, what she had said already to the police inspector, to the guide from the Château who had rushed out, to the group of uncomprehending tourists who had huddled round her.

'He was wearing eighteenth-century costume. A kind of loose blue silk shirt, all covered in ruffles, and breeches. His hair was all long and powdered, tied at the back of his head.'

'Only him? Not the man you saw attacking him?'

'All I took in was that he was wearing some white clothing - and he seemed to be wearing a *perruque*.'

Jean-Claude suddenly looked up from his note-taking.

'What?' asked Cecile. 'One of those eighteenth-century wigs?'

The girl said slowly, 'That's what it looked like, yes.'

'So was he wearing eighteenth-century costume?'

'I can't be sure, honestly. I'm trying to think - but it's as if my brain won't really remember, won't be forced to.'

There was a silence for a moment or two, broken by grinding gears heavily outside as a tourist bus moved past outside. As if sensing Marina's reluctance to add to what she had already said, Cecile Galant said patiently, 'There is something you must understand - a difference between the legal systems in France and England. My purpose is neither to prove guilt or innocence. I do not take sides. The *juge d'instruction* is to get at the truth of the matter, and for that reason I can enquire into any of the circumstances surrounding a crime. Or an alleged crime. Now, I would like you to tell me exactly what you are doing here in Versailles.'

Marina stared at her, seeking for some delay. She didn't want to tell this woman the truth. Because they would think there was something wrong, after what had happened in Woodstock. Although, of course, there wasn't. Nothing at all, really.

Chapter Eight

The apartment in the Boulevard Raspail was so stuffy. The dark shelves of books, the brown plush runner on the table, the turkey carpet - all seemed slightly dusty, though they had kept the windows shut against the hot August air, and the blinds were partly closed, slanting against the sun. There was a faintly disagreeable smell in the room, and the younger woman got up and stirred the bowl of pot-pourri on the mantelpiece, so that scents of lavender and carnation rose briefly before being conquered again by the stale air of Paris in August. Outside, a carriage clipped past: no doubt a tourist taken slowly round the city by a weary guide.

The younger woman was wearing a white dress, high-necked, with a fall of lace at the front; her fair hair was pinned up but strands were escaping and clung to her damp cheek. She walked to the window, drew up a corner of the blind to glance idly into the street, and took her place again at the table, where an open book awaited her, but glanced across the room rather than at its pages.

Sitting at a writing-table on the other side of the room was a woman with a strong, square face and deep-set eyes, her black hair streaked with grey at the temples. She was old enough almost to be the mother of the blonde woman, but there was no likeness at all between them: a stranger would have found no family relationship, though there were similarities of manner which might make one think that they shared some common preoccupations, by training and education, perhaps. Her head was bowed over the table. The force of her concentration seemed heavy in the room: the younger woman felt it almost as a physical barrier. She felt as if she were assessing her companion for the first time, seeing her through someone else's eyes - perhaps it was because they were abroad, two Englishwomen, away from home.

From the writing-table came the steady scratching of a pen on paper and the occasional tinkling tap of the metal nib against the glass of the inkpot, as the writer dipped in her pen and shook off the surplus drops.

The younger woman seemed restless.

'Would you like some tea, Annie - with lemon, perhaps? I could ring for Madeleine.' She spoke rather deferentially, as if anxious that she might upset her companion with the interruption.

The other woman shook her head. 'Really, what absurd names the French give their servants! No, thank you, Eleanor, I want to finish this letter.'

Eleanor went back to her book. But the small sounds of writing appeared to be intermittent, and in fact after a few more minutes they ceased altogether.

Annie had picked up her Bible.

'Let me read you our verses for the day.'

She began, in a loud, flat voice that seemed to fill the room.

'"And the woman was arrayed in purple and scarlet colour, and decked with gold and precious stones and pearls, having a golden cup in her hand full of abomination and filthiness of her fornications."'

The voice was monotonous, yet compelling.

Sometimes, thought Eleanor, it was almost as if Annie was possessed. Today, she didn't really want to listen, but there was no escaping, penned in as they were. It would be such a relief to go outside.

The voice continued, hypnotically. Eleanor found pictures forming and dissolving in her mind, of towers and gold crowns, and what else she could not well describe.

'"And he cried mightily with a strong voice, saying, Babylon the great is fallen, is fallen, and is become the habitation of devils, and the hold of every foul spirit, and a cage of every unclean and hateful bird.

'"For all nations have drunk of the wine of the wrath of her fornication and the kings of the earth have committed fornication with her, and the merchants of the earth are waxed rich through the abundance of her delicacies."'

The voice stopped.

Was it over for the day? Eleanor's mind was steadying, returning to the stuffy room, her hands gripping the blind-cord at the window as if automatically.

It seemed to have got much darker. Perhaps Annie would need more light to read. Did she, Eleanor, want her to go on? She wasn't sure, but at any rate, they needed some light in the room.

Eleanor turned to her companion, intending to ask if she wanted the lamps to be lit. But when she looked across the room, she saw that the other woman had put down her Bible and was gazing at her in a most strange manner, really, one might almost consider it ... well, her eyes were staring so oddly - Eleanor scarcely knew what to think, and wanted suddenly to cry out, to get up and leave the room, to look for someone else, anyone, another human being.

But she could hardly do that. She didn't want to upset Annie in any way.

They sat in silence for a few moments more.

Then Annie suddenly spoke.

'Do you think the Trianon is haunted?'

Chapter Nine

'No,' said Marina.'No.' She could still hear the bubbling sound that had come out of the young man's throat. 'He tried to speak. His lips were moving. I couldn't make out any words. Nothing.'

Nothing. It seemed such a terrible way for a human life to end - absurdly costumed and in the presence of an uncomprehending stranger struggling to control her own revulsion.

There was a pause. Marina felt herself trembling. She took a sip from the glass of water thoughtfully placed beside her elbow on the table. She had given them all the details she could remember, twice over, once to the policeman and once to this woman.

The woman seemed willing to change the subject; perhaps she sensed that breaking-point was close.

'So why did you come here, mademoiselle? Tell me about your visit to Versailles - not just to the Château.'

Marina said carefully, 'Well, of course, that's why I came. To see the Château.' For once in her life, she wanted to be just an ordinary muddled tourist, one among the flock, strung about with camera and flash, chivvied by a guide. 'Look no further,' she said silently, to the mind of the woman on the other side of the desk. 'I just happened to be in that place at that time. It could have been anyone - Mr. Mikado from Japan, or Mrs. Peanuts from Chicago, or Herr Lederhosen from the Tyrol. The whole world comes to see Versailles.'

The woman seemed to read her thoughts. 'Of course, everyone comes to see Versailles - that's what Louis XIV intended, after all!'

The small joke broke the ice, but did not put Marina at her ease, because Mme Galant went on quickly, 'But you, mademoiselle, you are not just another tourist, who comes here for an hour or two out from Paris. You are staying at your hotel for a week. So why was that?'

'I want to see a bit more than the average visitor, I suppose. I'm very interested in the art of the period.'

'Is that what you were studying? It is here, in your statement, that you are a student, working on a thesis.'

'Yes, well, it is about Versailles, though in the time of Louis XVI and Marie-Antoinette.'

Would the woman leave it at that?

No, she would not.

'So what are you investigating exactly, in this thesis? I would have thought that was a period very well examined by historians - though not, perhaps, in England?'

'Well, yes, I do want to have a new perspective ... it is not so much about Versailles itself, but more about its image, if you like, the way in which people have viewed it through the years ...'

'Ah, I understand. The symbol - what Versailles has represented, perhaps. The ultimate in wealth and luxury, a focus for social attack, and so on. But what else - that isn't very original, surely!'

She had seen the point straight away. That there must be something more.

'Yes, I was going to follow the theme into the nineteenth century, even into the early twentieth.'

She didn't want to say more. The chronology should be enough, surely. Her thesis had nothing to do with the events she had seen today.

But the woman didn't want to leave it alone. She leaned back in her chair, as though relaxed, but her brown eyes were very alert, and she seemed suddenly to be concentrating on something very intently. Marina was reminded of uncomfortable sessions with her supervisor, the sense of crossing swords with a very clever mind.

'And from whose point of view? The British?'

Damn the woman, why should she be so interested?

But they could find out quite easily. The French police could get the address where she had stayed in Paris, ask questions there. Even, she supposed, go to Oxford and ask around there. It would seem odder to try and hide it all than to tell them now.

'Well, yes ... that's right.'

Mme Galant leaned forward and examined some notes.

'You have been doing this research for - let me see - two years now. So you must have something definite. What is the precise topic?'

Had she noticed Marina's increasing nervousness?

'It's about something that occurred here a century ago. In the grounds. Near the Petit Trianon, the small pleasure Château.'

Near to where that terrible thing had happened, this very morning.

'Yes, go on.'

Anyway, thought Marina, it will take my mind off this image that keeps coming into it, that face, drained, contorted, trying to say something.

And then she wished fervently they'd found a body, and immediately realised what a dreadful thought that had been, that she should wish that a man had actually died rather than that she, Marina, might have imagined it. She tried to focus on the reason for her visit to Versailles in the first place.

'There were two English ladies, Miss Moberly and Miss Jourdain.'

The woman suddenly laughed aloud.

'Ah, yes, I have heard of them! It's a famous history, you know. If I remember correctly, they claimed to have seen ghosts at Versailles - isn't that the story? But you are not taking it seriously, surely?'

'No, of course not - that is, I don't think they saw the ghost of Marie -Antoinette and so forth. But historically, it is very interesting that Versailles should have been the focus for their fantasies. And many people have taken them quite seriously.'

Marina stopped, she didn't want to go on explaining anything. She certainly didn't want them to think she was some mad Englishwoman obsessed with supernatural goings-on. All she wanted to do was to get back to her room at the Auberge du Duc, and lie down. She had some of Dr. Basset's tablets in the drawer of her bedside table - a couple of those, and there would be a few hours of oblivion. Forgetting all about ghosts and death, about insubstantial August afternoons of a century ago, and the absurd blood-soaked reality of the present - she could still hardly believe in that. It seemed far more unreal than anything those two Victorian spinsters had imagined so long ago.

The woman was looking at her carefully, as if evaluating the situation.

'You were planning to stay in Versailles for a few more days?'

'Yes.'

'Then please do exactly that. You are free to return to your hotel, but there will be a police escort and a guard. We will want to speak to you again.'

Marina suddenly realised what she claimed to have seen: not only a murder, but the murderer. 'Oh, God,' she suddenly thought, a sickness grabbing her stomach again, and her mind was in a panic, so that she found she was saying it aloud; 'But he saw me, too! He saw me!'

'Yes, but you can feel quite secure - absolutely so. We can contact anyone you would like in England.'

Next of kin, thought Marina, they want to know in case ...

Aloud, she said, 'Well, my mother is on her own, and she's a bit frail - it's better if she doesn't know anything.'

'Anyone else?'

She gave them Luke's details, and those of her college, turning to spell the addresses out to the clerk, hearing the rhythmic tapping, the 'o's in 'Woodstock' and 'Oxford'.

'Very well, I'll have you driven back to your hotel. And if you have nothing better to occupy you, I would like you to do something. Make a summary of the incident of the two English ladies for me. I have heard about it, but I don't know any of the details. It's a matter of personal interest - put it like that.'

Mme Galant was standing up. As Marina got up to leave, she glanced down and saw for the first time that she had streaks of mud on her sleeves, and her inquisitor reached out and pointed to them.

'Where did the mud come from?'

Marina had forgotten the dying fish, gasping for air in the drained fountain beneath the golden statue. She tried to explain. It seemed so trivial and even foolish now, but the woman said gently, 'That was a kind thing to do,' almost as if she were applauding a good child.

She hadn't said anything about the scar, though she must have seen it. Sometimes Marina felt she didn't give a damn, and pushed back her hair almost deliberately, so that the long red ridge with the impeccably neat marks of the stitches and the shaven patch of short stubble around it was defiantly visible.

At other times, she couldn't bear it when people looked at her, the curious scrutiny, the surprised double-take, the unspoken questions. When she felt like that, she combed her hair carefully over the raw place, or sometimes wore the wig that lay even now at the bottom of her case in the room at the Auberge du Duc.

In any case, the scar would fade. But she didn't always believe that. Sometimes she felt she bore it for life. Was marked out by it, in fact.

What an odd thing, in a murder investigation, to ask her to write down the details of those Victorian English ladies and their 'ghosts' at Versailles! But Mme Galant was unusual anyway; surely no English magistrate or lawyer would be interested in these old histories. Still, the woman seemed to have remarkably perceptive eyes: Marina encountered her shrewd gaze, and felt uncomfortable, as if she had been unmasked in some way. But of course, it wasn't Marina who had put up a deception: more likely those pillars of society, Miss Moberly and Miss Jourdain.

The judge was saying something more.

'Mademoiselle, you must co-operate with us. Because the consequences for yourself may be very serious. You see -'

The judge leaned towards Marina and her voice now sounded very slow and careful.

'You see, there was no body.'

Chapter Ten

The grass of the Cathedral close seemed a brilliant emerald green in the summer morning. It was an hour or so after the dawn of what promised to be a beautiful summer's day. Beyond the grey stone walls, the needle-like spire rose precipitously up into a clear blue sky.

Within the high walls of the Bishop's private garden the dew lay still on the lawn and there was a curious absolute silence: no sounds came from the house beyond, not even the usual distant voices and clattering from kitchen or stables.

Then, suddenly, a woman rushed out of the house and into the sheltered enclosed space of the garden. She stood still and stared for a few moments, and then turned her face wildly up to the sky. She was no longer young, and it was a strange face, square-jawed, with protruding teeth, and deep-set black eyes beneath thick brows. Her hair was black and straight, coarse-textured and pulled back remorselessly from her forehead.

Then she began to run into the middle of the garden As she ran, clumsy, stumbling, she gasped and called out stray broken scraps. 'Dear God ... Thy will be done! ... Thy lamps are burning in heaven ... Glory, come glory!' She rubbed her eyes with stubby fingers, digging her nails into her cheeks as she dragged her hands down over them.

At the same time, sounds broke out around her: from the Cathedral beyond the high wall came the slow tolling of a deep bell, and from the house the muffled sounds of sobbing and the swishing sounds of heavy curtains pulled shut and windows slamming. The woman in the garden shrieked out and fell full length on the lawn, her black skirts falling heavily out like great shadows. She rolled over on to her back and lay staring up at the sky, as if pinned there like a monstrous black butterfly, the thin arms in tight-fitting sleeves bent at her sides like hooks.

A few minutes passed, during which she did not move.

From the house came another woman, small and anxious, her eyes wet with tears. She hurried across the lawn. 'Annie, this will do no good, you must get up! Mother needs us. Can you stand?' Pulling gently, she helped the other, unresisting, to stand up. The first woman clung to her for support, and babbled in her ear, 'I saw them, Alice, I saw them!'

She was led back, through the French windows and into a darkened room, where a shawl had been thrown over the piano and the curtains pulled close against the summer morning, but she did not stop the soft muttering. 'I saw them, two great white birds in the garden, and they spread their wings, with their feathers like snow! They were like albatrosses, gliding through the air, circling round and round. And then they took off and flew up, up into the sky, circling round and round till I couldn't see them any more! Oh, Alice, I saw the Bishop's birds! They come whenever the bishop dies, you know, it's an ancient legend. And I was a witness. God made me a witness!'

Alice put her arm round her sister and looked into the plain sallow face. 'Yes, yes it was a wonderful thing, but Annie -'

'It's true, Alice! I did see them, I did!'

'Yes, but Annie, listen to me. It's best if you don't say anything about it outside the family.'

'But why not? Don't you believe me?'

'Yes, yes, of course I believe you. But other people might not take it so, you know.'

Annie looked at her with a kind of angry bewilderment. But she said no more. A man had entered the room, dressed in black with the frock-coat and white collar of a clergyman. He looked inquiringly across to Alice as he walked towards the women, a worried frown on his thin features.

Annie called out, 'Robert, I saw the Bishop's birds! I did!'

'Hush, Annie!' said her sister, with a touch of hasty panic in her voice. 'Hush! The servants will hear.'

'Don't you believe me?'

Robert came towards her and spoke very softly, his voice almost swallowed up in the heavy fabrics that seemed to swaddle everything in the room. 'Yes, Annie, of course we believe you. But Alice is right. Let's not speak of it to other people - it would be better so. You may mention it in the family, if you wish- but I think not to outsiders, no, indeed.'

His youngest sister subsided on to a chair. 'Very well, Robert. If you wish. If you think best.'

'Yes, I do, Annie.' His voice was calm, firm, admitting no argument. 'It is best, for you and for the whole Moberly family, if from now on you keep your ... I know not what to say -'

'My visions.' There was a defiance in Annie's eyes, though she had always deferred to her brother.

'Yes, well, if that is what you want to call them. Keep them to yourself. Do you understand me, Annie?'

'Yes, Robert.'

Chapter Eleven

Marina had been driven back to the hotel in a police car, and was accompanied up to her room by a uniformed policewoman. The woman at the reception desk stared at her, but said nothing, asked nothing. Clearly, the hotel had been informed that she was now a special sort of guest, guarded or protected - which? She fumbled in her bag, her fingers shaking, handed the woman the room-key, and felt a deep sense of relief as the door swung open. This was her little space, for a few days, at any rate: her books on the bedside table, the bunch of flowers she had bought and placed in the glass from the bathroom in lieu of a vase.

No photographs. It was the first time she had travelled alone without a photograph of Luke.

The officer walked to the bathroom, glanced in, then stood in the middle of the room in her smart blue blouse and neat skirt, looking round efficiently. It was a small room: you could see everything from the one place.

'I just want to get some rest now,' said Marina, hoping she would be left alone at last. The policewoman moved to the door, saying, 'I'll be downstairs if you need me. If you feel hungry, we'll have something sent up to your room. Do you want anything now?'

'No, thank you.' But as soon as the woman had gone, Marina wished she had asked for a cup of tea, and picked up the bottle of mineral water beside her bed and drained it in thirsty gulps.

She lay on the single bed, closed her eyes, but couldn't sleep. There were images coming all the time, of a pale face and a gasping mouth, lips muttering something she kept bending to try and understand. His eyes had been huge, the brown irises glazed with bluish reflections, rolling upwards underneath the lids, the stupid blind expanse of veined white, like marbles, staring at her ... that had been the moment when she had vomited. Don't think about today. Think about the past, escape into it. It will keep you safe from the present.

What had happened at Versailles, in the gardens, one hundred years ago?

Marina got up and opened her case, taking out some sheets of paper, and went to the little dressing-table. She began to make notes and the beating in her heart subsided as she did so. They were calming, these old, long-gone things, distanced and apart from her.

The facts that were to be set out for the benefit of Cecile Galant were quite simple.

Chapter Twelve

Extracts from the notes of Marina Cassatt, made at Versailles, August 24th, 2000.

For Madame Galant, *juge d'instruction*, from Marina Cassatt

Two English ladies were walking in the grounds of Versailles on the afternoon of Saturday, August 10th, 1901.

In their photographs, they wear high-necked blouses tucked in at the waist with deep leather belts: somehow one is conscious of the heavy layers of clothing beneath, the petticoats that make for the thickness of the skirts.

They were of unimpeachable social respectability. The elder, Charlotte Anne Moberly, known to her family and friends as Annie, was a daughter of the late Bishop of Salisbury and the tenth of fifteen children. When the incident at Versailles took place, she was fifty-five years of age and Principal of St Hugh's College, Oxford. The younger, Eleanor Frances Jourdain, was thirty-eight, and, like her friend, the daughter of a clergyman, but a man of much lower standing, a Derbyshire vicar. The Jourdains, like the Moberlys, were one of those huge Victorian families: in her case, Eleanor was the eldest of ten children.

Annie Moberly, was educated at home, as was usual for many well-bred girls of her generation, presumably picking up bits of knowledge from a governess and from the atmosphere of a household formidably well-furnished with tomes of history and religion. The brothers were all sent away to school and destined for careers in the church or as schoolmasters. The entire family was musical, and sang psalms every morning.

Annie was a girl of great spiritual intensity who claimed to have seen the vision of 'the Bishop's birds', two white birds that were said to fly overhead when a Bishop died. She was considered a plain child, with a beautiful mother and elder sisters. No one expected her to marry well, or even to marry at all. She might well have remained at home for all of her life.

However, release from her expected destiny arrived unexpectedly. Elizabeth Wordsworth, a great-niece of the poet, was determined to found a women's college at Oxford. There were then only two such colleges, and Miss Wordsworth was already the Principal of one, Lady Margaret Hall. Like Annie Moberly, Elizabeth was the daughter of a Bishop, and wanted to create a foundation in memory of her father. Her father had been Bishop of Lincoln, and she determined to call the new college St. Hugh's, after the patron saint of Lincoln Cathedral.

Elizabeth Wordsworth needed a suitable woman as Principal for her new college. Although one might think that to be the head of an Oxford college required great intellectual achievement, this was not the case at that time: it was far more important to be an efficient administrator and of unimpeachable social and moral standing.

As the daughter of one Bishop, Elizabeth Wordsworth was acquainted with the clerical circle, and knew that in Winchester there was a suitable middle-aged candidate, left in poor circumstances by the death of her father. She was eminently qualified because of her family background and her religious soundness. At Lady Margaret Hall, much was made of claims that the college had 'the ways and tone of a Christian family' and the same would be true of St. Hugh's.

Many of the women who were educated at these institutions were of remarkably strong intellects and personalities: they had to be, because there was often great opposition, at home and in society generally, to the whole idea that women should receive university education. Their minds were generally considered inferior to those of men, and the whole exercise of higher education to be a subversion of their natural destiny of marriage and motherhood, even morally dubious. So anxious were the first women's colleges to prove that their students were paragons of virtue that a rigid, paralytic desire for respectability on the part of the college authorities fastened women in Oxford into shackles that elsewhere were being broken. The students were accompanied by chaperones everywhere they went.

Annie Moberly, however, would never want to break free. In that respect, she was a very safe choice for the first principal of St. Hugh's: the job was really that of a very upper-class housekeeper and moral guardian.

It does not seem very clear how Miss Jourdain came to be offered the post of Vice-Principal of St. Hugh's College. She was better educated than Annie Moberly, having studied at Lady Margaret Hall, so she also would have been well known to Miss Wordsworth. In any event, both women, Miss Moberly and Miss Jourdain, had mutual friends in the small circle of educated women from clerical backgrounds in which they moved.

Eleanor Jourdain had also demonstrated considerable initiative and organisational ability. Determined to be more than an ordinary schoolmistress after leaving Oxford, she founded her own school, the Corran School in Hertfordshire, which aimed at giving a genteel but thorough education to well-brought-up young ladies. She was making a good success out of this venture when Miss Moberly offered her the post of Vice-Principal of St. Hugh's.

Eleanor had continued with academic work, studying Dante. But her ambitions also led her to France. Her family was of Huguenot stock, and she became fluent in the language, though she did not visit France till she was thirty years of age, and did not see Paris till she was thirty-six, in the year before the Versailles adventure. At her school, she employed a French teacher, Mlle Jeanne Ménégoz, whose father was Professor of Theology at the Sorbonne, and with Mlle Ménégoz, Miss Jourdain acquired an apartment in Paris, where they planned to take small groups of the older girls, to give them a little cultural polish and receive extra coaching in French. It was a commercial venture which also gave her a pied à terre in Paris.

When Miss Moberly invited her to become Vice-Principal, the two ladies decided first to spend a few weeks in this flat in Paris, before Miss Jourdain committed herself definitely to moving to Oxford.

This delay seems strange. Was Miss Moberly unconsciously the wooer and Miss Jourdain the elusive wooed who will not give an answer? Miss Jourdain was very unlikely to actually refuse the offer of the post in Oxford, for it represented a great opportunity for her, though her school was proving a success. It might well have been that she wanted to keep Miss Moberly waiting a little for a definite response.

In any event, during the visit to Paris they decided to make an excursion to Versailles and something happened there that affected the whole course of their future lives. It was the first time either of them had visited the Château. Perhaps what they claimed to find there made up Miss Jourdain's mind; perhaps, in a sense, it was a way of providing Miss Moberly with her answer.

Chapter Thirteen

'Come on, I want to take you somewhere.'

Marie and Toni were in the smoky bar, some distance behind the Chantiers station. Outside was a brilliant afternoon sky. He was looking into her eyes, stroking his finger on the inside of her thigh. No one round their table cared.

She knew she'd had too much to drink, but it just seemed to make her want him more. They were out on to the street, laughing, and then on the bike, trees slipping past.

'It makes me dizzy - where we goin'? To that place you were on about?'

'I'll show you. It's special.'

She felt nervous, without knowing why, but he bent down to her and said, 'It's going to be all right - you'll see.'

'You're not angry?'

His eyes opened wide. She had read somewhere in a magazine that meant people were telling the truth. If they lied, they screwed up their eyes. That's what it had said.

So she looked specially and his light-coloured eyes, with their long black lashes, were wide open as he said, 'Angry, no, of course not! I didn't expect it, that's all.'

'I could do something about it, you know. I just have to arrange it. It's happened before ... Funny, this time, with you, I want to keep it. I've never felt like that before.'

'Well, you're with me, now.'

Relaxing, feeling some great tension breaking up inside her like ice cracking on a river, she climbed on behind him and clutched his back, warm and smooth, and the bike roared off, the wind rushing at them as they tore along.

She hadn't been anywhere like it before. Outside the town, they turned off, away from any proper roads, and the bike bounced along a track so that the breath was almost knocked out of her a couple of times and she had to hang on tighter than ever. She wanted to get him to stop or slow down, at any rate, but it was useless the wind and the vibration were whipping away all her shouts, and there were no signals she could give that he would understand, no nudges or taps. But when he finally roared to a halt, she stared around wonderingly. Surrounded by trees, distant from anywhere tourists were likely to wander, it was a tiny lodge, perched at the edge of a park, which had once, before the Revolution, been part of the grounds of the Château. The miniature house was so pretty, like an old picture, the grass and bushes all overgrown around it, with only a track leading round the house.

Her arms were aching a bit from clinging on, but she walked towards the place like someone in a dream. There was an absolute silence, deeper than she could have imagined, with only the song of a bird somewhere close by.

Toni went straight up to the door, but Marie said on an impulse, 'Let's walk around it first. I don't want to go inside yet.'

The red brick walls and tall windows were bathed in the sunshine. There was an overgrown yard at the back, with an old pump and a stable. 'That's the only water', he said.

'Does it work?'

'Yeah. Tried it. Water tastes OK.'

They walked on, through the tangles of shrubbery and herbiage that had once been lawns, and got back to the front, where the bike stood incongruously, the air around it shimmering still with heat.

Inside, there was just one big room, with a fireplace and some sort of stone sink in a corner, and a stair-case leading up to a big dusty attic with little windows in the roof. There were a couple of narrow mattresses in a corner, and a blanket, nothing else.

Looking out of the nearest window, she could see a string of horses passing under distant trees, their steady movement the only sign of life.

'Oh, Toni, it's lovely here!'; she said. 'You never told me about it.'

It didn't seem his kind of place, but she thought it was so beautiful that she didn't worry about that. 'Who does it belong to?' she asked.

'Oh, a friend. He'll let me have it rent free as long as I keep an eye on things.' He squeezed her arm. 'I fixed it all specially for us.' His lips nibbled her ear. She giggled. 'It must be the hormones!' she said, as he felt how wet she was between her thighs.

In fact, the hut - it could have been called by some fancy name, a lodge, a garden-house, perhaps - belonged to an old woman, who had inherited it along with several other privately-owned places scattered round the skirts of the great expanse of parkland, once the private domain of the king. Toni, bombing his moto-bike away from the town and through the alien forest, was looking for somewhere on the edge of things, somewhere partly hidden, for reasons in himself he didn't understand at the time. But there were reasons which he did recognise, and saw as practical, such as the necessity to lie low. He had cruised past it one day, and realised it was abandoned.

A park-keeper had told him the address of the owner. It was easy to persuade the old woman into letting him live there. It would have been difficult to let, since it had been built as an ornamental structure, a little summer play-cottage. The fireplace and a pump in the yard were the extent of the amenities.

Besides, Toni had put on his charmer act, told the old lady he had been ill and was looking for a bit of peace and quiet. He would guarantee to put the place in good repair.

This counted for a lot, as it was fast crumbling, and Toni had indeed fixed a few tiles on the roof and replaced a couple of rotting floorboards. He had to, in order to make it habitable at all.

But there he stopped, though he felt, that first day when the old lady had fetched the huge iron key and he had turned it in the lock, a huge sense of satisfaction: this was his own, secret space. There was one large room downstairs, with a sink in one corner, and an incongruously wide staircase, the winding hand-rail now roughened and splintered in places. There was no partitioning into rooms upstairs, either: just the one long low stretch under the roof, with the dirty old panes letting in a cool green light filtered through the neighbouring trees.

Anyone else would have thought it beautiful. Toni did feel a powerfully strong sensation, an exultation. It was as though this place was the start of something for him, yet of something he had always wanted, deep down, for a long time.

He didn't normally like old things. The cement walls and walkways of the block of Paris flats in which he had been brought up, and where his early drug-dealing had been conducted, had been neutral for him. He neither liked nor loathed them, he could do nothing to change anything about them, and that was that.

Old places, he thought, were different. They did do something to you. You had to think about them sometimes, think about what had happened there. They could put ideas in your head.

Of course, there were things not so attractive about the place. There was a shed with a hole in the ground for a bog.

And there was the cellar.

Anyone else would have been repelled by the cellar.

Toni most definitely was not.

He had thought for a few moments it was all spoilt, ruined, when she told him about the kid.

She could always get rid of it, like she said. But she didn't want to, he could tell.

'Toni, it would be lovely for a kid here! All the greenery and the birds and everything.'

In a way, this place made it clear, the difference between them.

He didn't believe the kid was his, anyway. She was trying to trap him, that was all. He didn't want it here, not in his private place. He didn't know what he wanted this house for, but not to have a bloody kid running round. No, he wanted it for something quite different. What, he didn't know, yet, but he wasn't going to have it spoiled.

But he could always think of a way out. He used to trap small creatures - insects, if he could get nothing bigger - and shut them in, and watch them try to get out, probing blindly helplessly, as he watched. Stupid, he thought, stupid creatures.

Yes, he, Toni, could always get out of things.

Even out of this thing she had done to him.

Chapter Fourteen

Although Colas, the senior police officer, was plump, he was a heavy smoker, and the smell of cigarette smoke was always hanging round after he left and filling Cecile's small office. It made her want to start smoking again. She took a few deep breaths close to the open window and filled her lungs with something cleaner.

As he went out, she buzzed on her intercom.

'Jean-Paul? I'm ready for them now.'

Two men entered the room, one of them in the formal black lawyer's robe, with the traditional white neckband. He was a florid-faced plump character, whom Cecile had already encountered a few times. Maître Joseph, a leading advocate for the defence, who had won a series of notable cases. But not of this nature. What's he doing here, thought Cecile, with a client arraigned on a petty charge like this?

The lawyer's client was in his late fifties, she thought, his nose high-beaked and his chin held up ramrod-straight. A military bearing, presumably, learned many years ago as a cadet at Saint-Cyr, the nearby officers' academy, nursery of France's most famous warriors. The face was grey, the eyes reddened and watering. His hair was silver, thinning and sleeked back, untidier than one might expect in such a personage.

They sat down on the uncomfortable little chairs. Before Cecile could say anything, Maître Joseph said immediately, 'My client will plead not guilty.'

Cecile sat back and took a deep breath in the face of this idiocy. Presumably Maître Joseph was strictly following his client's instructions, but even he could not hope to bring this one off. Under her hand lay the file, the evidence of guilt piled as thick as the evidence for innocence had been thin.

A delay would be a good thing. Might make this man realise the folly of his position, the waste of everyone's time which a plea of 'Not Guilty' would be.

She sat for a few minutes, saying nothing. The lawyer gazed blandly back, but his client shuffled his thin hams on the chair. He was staring now at a point somewhat above her head. Perhaps it was some trick they taught them at S. Cyr. 'Don't look the enemy in the eye - unnerve him with your unwavering stare into space!'

Except that she was a woman, and anyway, as a human being, not officer material.

She continued to wait. Eventually, the Marquis de Vouet gave an aristocratic sniff.

'Could we have a window open?'

Must be the smell of Colas' cheap tobacco still hanging in the air. Not used to that, I suppose, thought Cecile, but she saw that Vouet's tweeds were old, that his shirt collar looked frayed. Member of the upper classes, gets an expensive lawyer, but fallen on hard times? Maybe it was family connections, not money, that had brought this smooth Paris lawyer running to Versailles with a preposterous plea.

She gestured to Jean-Claude and the clerk moved to one of the high windows and pulled it open. Jean-Claude sat down again.

Vouet shuffled some more.

Cecile opened the file and began reading. She made no acknowledgement of the presence of the accused and his lawyer.

After a few minutes, she looked up and saw that Vouet had now condescended to look at her.

'A petty victory,' she thought.

She began.

'You are Antoine Philippe Hugo de Vouet?

'I am the Marquis de Vouet, yes.'

Head held high, nasal voice, unquavering.

It might have been an interrogation before a revolutionary tribunal, with the tumbril waiting outside to take him to the guillotine. Cecile almost longed to call him 'citizen'. He would be 'Citizen Vouet', as the deposed King Louis XVI was known as the Citizen Capet.

I mustn't play his game, thought Cecile. He's not going to be allowed to make a martyr of himself. The evidence is absolutely unequivocal.

Aloud, she said, 'The charge against you is theft.'

'I am not guilty!'

Cecile said patiently, 'There is a CCTV film which shows you taking a mirror out of the department store. You are clearly recognisable. The mirror was under your coat. You were stopped by the store detective, and were unable to produce a receipt.'

'I had put it on my store account.'

'You should still have had a receipt.'

'I must have dropped it. Or the shop assistant forgot to give it to me.'

'And the store has no record that you put the mirror on your account.'

'Lazy and inefficient! These people -'

Maître Joseph made a warning noise in his throat, no sort of word, a sound impossible to enter in the record that Jean-Claude was making of the interview, yet effective in deterring his client from the dangerous course of abusing potential witnesses.

Cecile continued.

'And the mirror was unwrapped.'

Triumphantly, the Marquis countered this, leaning forward, pressing his hands on his bony, tweedy knees.

'That was why I put it under my coat. In case it rained.'

All parties seemed to pause at this point. Jean-Claude, pausing in his note-taking, gave a suspiciously snorting sound and hastily buried his nose in a handkerchief. Maître Joseph seemed to be keeping his face absolutely impassive: only his eyes, upturned towards the heavens, suggested untold realms of legal despair.

Cecile saw it was hopeless. She was torn between laughter and irritation.

'Very well, I will record that you have stated categorically that you are not guilty, and your case will come to court in due order.'

She must have betrayed impatience in her voice, for the Marquis leaned over the desk and said angrily, his voice now high-pitched,

'This accusation is a disgrace - and you, madame, seem to have judged me already! I cannot believe the types who seem to be in charge nowadays! Do we no longer believe that men are presumed innocent till proven guilty?'

Cecile was conscious of her own anger now, but sought deliberately now to keep her voice controlled and impersonal. Besides, this gave her an opportunity for a magnificent put-down.

'Of course we do. The presumption of innocence has been part of the French constitution since the Declaration of the Rights of Man in 1789.' There was a chilly irony in her voice. She might as well have said, 'Since your ancestors had their heads chopped off during the Revolution.'

The lawyer intervened, deliberately not catching her eye, then turning his head and carefully studying the ceiling. She sensed that behind her Jean-Claude might still be having trouble keeping a straight face.

'Madame le juge, my client will formally plead not guilty to the charge. Will you continue to allow him bail?'

Yes, she would, and Jean-Claude made the necessary record.

As they left, Cecile tried to consider the matter dispassionately. It was an odd incident, for a respectable personage of his age, after all. In a middle-aged woman accused of shoplifting, Cecile might well have considered that a psychiatric report would be desirable.

She dismissed it from her mind. There were too many cases on her list to worry about such a minor matter.

Chapter Fifteen

Daniel walked through the park with the child. Florence was not his, yet since his marriage to Cecile, he had grown to love, as well as to feel responsible for, this offspring of his wife's first marriage. The little girl was dancing at the end of his arm and then let go suddenly and ran off, to stand peering up into the branches. Above her fair head, he saw a dark shape darting through the oak leaves.

'It's a squirrel, Daniel!'

'He can't be getting ready for the winter - it's too early.'

'He's just playing, I think. Look, there he goes!'

They walked on as the squirrel scampered away from them. Daniel looked down at Florence's neat little face, with her tiny pink mouth, a mouth which in the nineteenth-century would have been likened to a rose-bud. They moved on, and the great trees spread their branches overhead, the trunks thick and gnarled and covered with patches of velvety moss. Some of the trees had probably been here for centuries, thought Daniel, and had looked down on the fêtes and gallantry below.

'Daniel, I like it here. Better than in the South.'

'Why's that?'

'I can go out more.'

'Yes, I know. It's good, isn't it?' The reason for this paradox, the sense of freedom that living in the wet and chilly north of France had given to all of them, was quite simple, but Daniel, of course, could not explain it to the seven-year-old Florence. It was that they were no longer under round-the-clock police protection from the revenge of the gangster, White Boy, and his thugs who still spread their tentacles along the southern coast. During her throughgoing investigation of the murders committed by the Cannes Mutilator, Cecile had also uncovered enough evidence to put White Boy in jail for a very long time. It had been a long case, complicated by the presence of the Englishman, Charlie Cashel, whose sister had been killed in Cannes, but eventually Cecile and Inspector Maubourg had between them unravelled all the complex threads. Though it had not done their professional reputations much good, since the civic authorities in Cannes, the most glamorous tourist trap on the Côte d'Azure, would much rather have kept the lid on the whole affair.

But at any rate, Cecile was now out of the reach of White Boy and his thugs or at least, out of their range of interest. No longer a juge d'instruction in a Riviera town, where she daily confronted their threats and bribery. Here at Versailles, her stubborn probity, irritating to some, could do no harm.

It had been a good move, thought Daniel, though Florence's father, Louis, that pompous stuffed shirt of a notary, had objected loudly and strenuously at first. His parents lived in Provence, his daughter could go and live with them, she would be perfectly safe, it was just that being with her mother put her in danger.

It had taken a personal visit from a senior policeman, Chief Inspector Maubourg, before Louis had been persuaded that his daughter was really threatened. Daniel remembered how Maubourg had called round to see them afterwards, and stood in the middle of the room swearing with exasperation at the man's obtuseness. 'Really, I would never have thought - he just totally failed to see the point! In the end, I said to him, do you want your daughter to be killed? Because that's what will happen if one of White Boy's friends gets hold of her, now that Madame has managed to get him put in jail.'

And Daniel had wondered himself at the thought of Louis's stupidity: the most notorious gangster in the South of France was unlikely to let any opportunity of leverage or revenge pass him by. Didn't he realise that?

'Of course he should,' said Cecile once, when they were discussing it with Pierre Maubourg.'But Louis doesn't think like that.' The two men looked at her in surprise. 'He thinks about property,' she continued, 'he thinks about his parents' land, about the family mas built of stone by his ancestors. And his daughter is part of that property - it's all immovable, rooted in the soil of Provence. It's about ownership, you see.'

But now they had been in Versailles for six months, and there had been no sign of any trouble: no shadowy figures following them through the streets, no taps on the telephone, nothing and noone lurking in Cecile's office. The transfer, outwardly a normal move, had been successful. And certainly, for the child, it was better out here than in central Paris, or some industrial northern town. As for Daniel himself, there might be the chance of a job at the University of Saint-Quentin nearby. He had plenty of web-designing work coming in, anyway.

When they got home, Cecile was already there, getting some lemonade out of the refrigerator. Florence ran ahead of him and Cecile's face lit up. 'Hello, darling! You want some?'

She poured out glasses from the jug, which had an icy layer over its curved surface. They all three drifted out into the little garden, where there were chairs set under a chestnut tree. The tree was too big for the garden, in truth, but Cecile loved its shade. After the heat of Cannes, the sheltering green coolness of the north was still a delight.

Florence went to play on the swing, singing to herself. She was a self-sufficient child, imaginative, Cecile, thought, amusing herself, but that was a bit worrying, too. Perhaps the child was too solitary.

'Do you think Florence should have more friends? We don't really know anyone here yet.'

'She'll make friends at school, don't worry.'

Daniel perched on one of the garden chairs and said, looking up at the thick green branches above him, 'You know, there are some really ancient trees round here - we went past some today that must have practically have been here in the days of the Sun King himself! Here, you can't get away from the past! At least in Cannes there was no history!'

'You sound very cynical!' said Cecile, and laughed. 'You can't escape it in Versailles, that's true. That English girl - the student who said she witnessed a murder, the one I told you about. She's doing some research into those two English spinsters who thought they had gone back in time - you know the ones I mean?'

Daniel was intrigued.

'No, I don't think I've ever heard of them. What happened?'

'Well I can't remember much. They claimed to have seen ghosts around the Petit Trianon, and they wrote a book to prove it, I think, claiming they had seen things they couldn't have known about beforehand.'

'So they couldn't have made them up?'

'That was the general idea'

'But that girl you interviewed, she can't believe it, surely? Or if she does ...'

'Then she's a crazy, and a thoroughly unreliable witness! Yes, I suppose it fits with the picture of her as a hysterical person - a fantasist. But she said she was approaching it as a historical episode, and that could make sense. The women were apparently rational, you know, they were quite important people at home. Something to do with Oxford University.'

'What about her - the girl? Do you think you can trust what she says?'

'I'm being honest, darling, I don't know. She claimed to see a crime being committed in the grounds of the Château, but there's no trace that anything of the sort happened. I think Dumont will want me to dismiss it out of hand, maybe even charge her with raising a false alarm or something of the sort, and I can't say I blame him.'

'No, after all, it must have wasted quite a lot of police time.'

'But I asked her to do something,' Cecile continued, 'to write out an account of the ghost story for me. It'll give me a chance to assess her mentality - how objective she is about it.'

Daniel laughed. 'You always have an ulterior motive!'

'Not always.' She leaned over and kissed his mouth.

The phone was ringing.

'Damn,' said Cecile and got up reluctantly. She went indoors to the long cool room, decorated in a silvery grey, where shadowy pools of bluish light came through the tall windows. The narrow old floorboards had almost a velvety look, so rubbed had they become with time. Cecile loved them, and had insisted they put only a few scattered rugs here and there in the big ground-floor apartment, converted from one of the old eighteenth-century houses. It accorded well with Daniel's taste for modernism: for furniture, they had acquired various structures in perspex, steel and natural wood, which actually fitted more elegantly into their surroundings than did the fussy 'Louis-Quinze' which seemed to obsess most people who moved into these old Versailles houses. 'The real thing's just down the road', Daniel has said, waving in the direction of the Château. 'Why try to compete?'

Now, picking up the phone and rubbing a toe absent-mindedly into the brilliant red and indigo splash of their Heriz rug, she was glad of Daniel's taste.

'Madame Galant?'

The voice was familiar, but it took her a moment or two to recognise it.

'It's Pierre Maubourg here, from Cannes.'

'Oh, hello!' She hadn't seen him for what? - the best part of a year. 'Are you calling from Cannes, Inspector.'

'No, madame, I'm in the district, as a matter of fact - by chance I had to come to Paris, so I thought I'd give you a call.'

There was more. She knew Maubourg. This was just a cue.

'Why don't you come out and have dinner with us? -It'll only be half an hour or so. Plenty of trains from St-Lazare, or there's the line south of the Seine. And we live right in the centre of town.'

She gave him directions, regretting the loss of the evening alone with Daniel, hoping he couldn't hear the regret in her voice.

'Maubourg's coming,'she said as she stepped out again into the garden.

'What's he want - just a social call?'

'No,' she said, thoughtfully, picking up her lemonade and sliding her fingers round the cool glass, 'No, it didn't sound quite like that.'

'Perhaps he wants to cry on your shoulder about - what's her name? Violetta?'

'I don't think so,' she answered absent-mindedly, thinking about possibilities. 'No, he would never say anything about her - he's very proud, you know. No, it must be something else.'

Chapter Sixteen

Further extracts from the notes of Marina Cassatt, made at Versailles, August 24th, 2000.

They wrote it down. But not straight away - that's the odd thing. Three months later, in November, 1901. They wrote out their accounts separately then, but they must have talked about what had happened - or seemed to have happened. And they didn't publish their stories for another decade, though they talked about it to their friends. When their book came out, it was called, 'An Adventure.' It was probably the only adventure either of them admitted to in the entire course of their lives.

It was about four o'clock on an oppressive August afternoon. They had seen the Château, and walked out of the rear entrance into the gardens, and down the central avenue, in the direction of the Trianons, those luxurious miniature palaces. Miss Moberly and Miss Jourdain especially wanted to see the smaller of the two, the Petit Trianon, famous because of its association with Marie-Antoinette. The Queen had commissioned architects to design gardens around it and a theatre inside, and had studded the grounds with charming miniature temples and follies in classical taste, and with waterfalls and rockeries.

The two ladies strolled along, taking the longest way round. They had a guide-book - Baedeker, of course, the universal companion for cultured British travellers. They were chatting about friends in England as they walked, so they claimed afterwards.

They came to a building on their left which they identified as the Grand Trianon, an elegant eighteenth-century construction with a distinctive long colonnade, and passed beyond it. Further along, Miss Moberly saw a woman shaking a cloth into the driveway from the doorway of a building on the right. Ahead, there was a country lane, and Miss Jourdain led the way along it. They thought they had gone too far and turned sharply to the right: Miss Moberly said that from this point on a frightful depression came over her, which she could not shake off. They passed some deserted buildings. Then they walked on, and the path seemed to go upwards, with rough ground on one side. They saw two men, from whom they asked the way, who were dressed in greyish-green coats and small three-cornered hats: one of them was holding a spade, so they made the reasonable assumption that the men were gardeners. The men directed the ladies straight on.

The path they were following joined another, which crossed it from left to right, and at this point Miss Moberly felt the sensation of gloom become overpowering. Before them was a slope leading down to a stream, which to their right was crossed by a rustic bridge. To the left was a little classical-style temple standing on an island in a miniature lake, which they thought was the Temple de l'Amour, shown in their guidebooks, a pretty columned rotunda with a statue of Venus and Eros. Miss Moberly said later that nothing would have induced her to turn left: she felt that everything, even the trees in the woods behind the Temple, seemed flat and one-dimensional, as if it were worked in tapestry. She afterwards also said that she had experienced extraordinary sensations of being closed in, and of deathly stillness.

On the balustrade of the temple sat a man, who looked towards them. He had a repulsive, scowling, face. Another man ran up towards them, coming over a rock or something similar where the path went off to their left. This was a tall handsome man, red in the face, breathless, with dark eyes, and wearing a sombrero-type hat. He urged them to go to the right, and they did so, crossing the little bridge. They went around a house, a square stone house with a terrace running round it. There were long windows closed with shutters at the back of the house and a lady was on a seat on the lawn, either sketching or reading. When they passed her, she turned and looked at them: Miss Moberly described her face as not young, and rather pretty, though not attractive. She was wearing a white straw hat on top of her fair hair. She had a light summer dress, with an arrangement like a handkerchief over the shoulders, with a little line of green or gold near the edge of the handkerchief. The dress seemed to be short in front, but Miss Moberly was not sure about this. She had a sheet of paper in her hand, which Miss Moberly thought was blank. The latter thought the lady's expression had something unattractive in it and she turned away.

The two English ladies went onto the terrace, and Miss Moberly saw the lady again from behind, and noted that the handkerchief arrangement, which she now called a muslin fichu, was pale green. Miss Moberly thought at the time that she was a tourist, and wondered that she was sitting in a place which seemed to be dark and dreary.

Then a young man emerged from a doorway and said that the two ladies had to enter the house from the front, and directed them down another path. This one was parallel with the path on which they had met the gardeners. He walked along with them, with an amused expression. They came to the opening leading into the drive that went past the front entrance, where they found a large French wedding party, joined the group and went inside the house with them, where they walked through the rooms.

Miss Jourdain's experiences were somewhat different, as she afterwards recorded them. She saw a gate leading to the country lane or path, which she described as being set deep below the level of the surrounding ground, the gardeners seen by Miss Moberly, and a woman and a girl coming out of a building like a farmhouse. The girl was holding a mug. The buildings seemed deserted and implements were lying around. At the building which they thought was the Temple de l'Amour, she saw the man seated on the balustrade and noted that he had a heavy black cloak and a slouch hat. At that point, she found that an eerie feeling had turned into an impression of something very uncanny, and she was deeply afraid. The man turned his face towards them; it looked very evil, but he did not seem to see them. Then another man, a fellow with a florid complexion, came running along from behind them, and called out to turn to the right, and not to the left. He was youngish, and his hair was rather long and dark. Miss Jourdain thanked him, and he ran off with an odd smile on his face. The two ladies found themselves at the garden frontage of the Petit Trianon.

And that, basically, was that. But on this slender foundation they built an entire castle in the air: it became a mutual obsession which occupied them for a quarter of a century, till Eleanor Jourdain died, and afterwards Annie Moberly, who survived her by thirteen years, was unable to relinquish this curious passion. It became the most famous ghost story in history. For they claimed no less than that they had stepped back into the past and experienced it through the mind of a ghost.

Chapter Seventeen

'But of course, it's not history,' said Daniel. 'Just the fantasies of a couple of English spinsters. Very Freudian, don't you think? The gate leading to the deep-cut path - well, that's pretty obviously the hymen. The handsome man, red in the face, breathless - surely a Freudian would say it's the circumstances of the primal scene, the child witnessing the sexual act. But I don't understand how it came to be so important, this whole episode.'

'They were such respectable women, I suppose,'said Cecile, flicking through Marina Cassatt's notes. 'And they couldn't leave it alone. According to Marina Cassatt, no sooner had they got back to England than they started telling everybody about it - and it got more and more embroidered. They ended up claiming that the woman Miss Moberly saw was Queen Marie-Antoinette!'

'Good God,' said Daniel. 'But I'm not surprised. People have turned her into a tragic heroine, and it's not surprising if they focus a lot of fantasies around her. Swanning around on lawns in gorgeous silk skirts, bravely facing the guillotine after the Revolution, that's the mental picture everyone has of her.'

'Yes. Miss Moberly was writing about what they had seen from the apartment in the Boulevard Raspail, apparently. And the two women they kept claiming that various details were proved true - that things they couldn't have known about before were proved historically correct, I mean. But there seems to have been a tremendous amount of suggestion entering into it. The lady Miss Moberly saw sitting in the garden - it was only after Mademoiselle Ménégoz told them that there had been stories about the ghost of Marie-Antoinette being seen at the Trianon that they decided it must have been the Queen - and then the Moberly woman claimed to recognise the face in a portrait of Marie - Antoinette. Very poor identification evidence - the description she gave before she saw the picture of the Queen could have been almost anybody.'

'And Jourdain didn't see her at all?'

'No, but she totally accepted Moberly's version.'

'Hmm. Anyway, it's interesting, I suppose, psychologically.'

'It's a relief from the other stuff. It's as nasty here as anywhere else - I don't know why I expected it to be better. Just the image of Versailles, I suppose, where courtiers were bending and bowing and dressing up in silks. But people maim and kill here as much as anywhere else on the face of the earth, perhaps more, really, when you think about all the statesmen who have met here. It's still an important place for entertaining visiting politicians, after all, they keep a suite in the Château for them. These two, Moberly and Jourdain - it all seems so innocent. Another age altogether. Perhaps that's why I enjoy reading about it.'

There was a chime from the direction of the front door and Daniel went to open it. She heard his voice in the hallway and then he ushered Maubourg into the room. Their greetings were friendly, yet with a certain tension and formality, as of two people who have worked together, respect each other, like each other, yet need to keep a professional distance, men who have their private lives.

Daniel poured drinks.

'We're just having something simple for dinner', he said, handing Maubourg the glass of chilled beer he had asked for. 'I'll go and ask Florence to help me lay the table.'

'My daughter has grown!' Cecile was smiling. 'She's very good at doing things like setting the table - she likes putting everything where it has to go.'

'And telling me when I've got it wrong', joked Daniel. Their dining-room was next door, and Cecile and Maubourg could hear their voices occasionally, Daniel's deeper rumbles interspersed with the child's high-pitched voice, and the frequent bursts of laughter from both of them. 'How good it sounds', said Maubourg. 'To hear them laughing like that, I mean.' He looked suddenly embarrassed and Cecile said quickly, 'How is Cannes?'

He didn't waste time. 'I have to tell you this personally.'

She sat up suddenly, seeing the look on his face, dark and anxious.

'He's in jail', she said. 'We put him away. For directing the attack on the house in Provence.'

That attack when Maubourg had killed a murderer with his bare hands, and his men had intercepted that bloated spider who sat at the centre of a network of drug-dealing and murder, employing psychopaths and rewarding them with victims. White Boy, who never went out into the fierce, cleansing sun of the South of France, and now sat shut away from the sun behind prison walls.

'He's in Lyons.'

'It's been modernised, Lyons, hasn't it?'

'Yes - the cells are new. Though it has three times the numbers it should have. 'He remembered the overcrowding, the men piled into tiny spaces, the stink. 'But he's in a separate block.'

'Privilege?'

'Or fear of corruption. Anyway, he hasn't given up. He's set someone on to you, madame.'

'Me, in particular?' Her face looked tense, but she stayed calm. She always did, he remembered.

'It seems he's taken it particularly badly, to have been trapped by a woman.'

'How did you get the information?'

'A contact who came out of Le Mans.'

This was the prison where accused men were held, awaiting trial. A clearing-house for rumour, as prisoners waited their fate, and some of that rumour drained into the outside world with those who occasionally escaped the system and emerged into the comparatively clean air of the outside world. Montvallon, Maubourg's sidekick in Cannes, had collared a little grubby thief in a hotel on the Croisette, caught him red-handed. Later, in the police station, the dirty, shrunken-looking face had twisted suddenly round, as if fearful of being overheard even at this distance, by a fat creature squatting in a cell in Lyon. But the fear of returning to prison, this time without walking free, had prompted a trade.

White Boy had set a contract out for a woman, Montvallon learned. Not just some ordinary tart. The person who had really put him away, not the prosecutor, not the trial judge. The woman who had directed the investigation that had resulted in this unspeakable ignominy of his imprisonment. The juge d'instruction, the examining magistrate, Cecile Galant.

The little man was released. Montvallon knew he could easily lay hands on him again - and would.

What he didn't know was that the next time he would be laying hands on a corpse. The stunted body was washed up at the foot of the cliffs. The corpse was battered, but that could have been from the pounding of the waves. Naked, but it could have been stripped by the powerful currents and the tearing of the sharp rocks. Marked, on the hands, feet and body, with a deliberate and careful tattoo pattern of cigarette burns. For these last good reasons, Maubourg believed that the little man had told the truth to les flics.

Maubourg didn't tell Cecile this. It would be enough to warn her, he thought. She would know what the odds were - she didn't need it spelling out.

'You're warning me?'

'Yes.'

'And official channels? The police here at Versailles? They haven't contacted me.'

'I've informed them. But I wanted to put you on your guard. Make sure you were really aware of the danger.'

He didn't add that the attitude of the police judiciaire at Versailles, to whom the threat had been reported, had seemed very unwilling to take it very seriously.

'Judges get threats all the time, Chief Inspector. We can't keep a round-the-clock guard on all of them.'

'Not on all of them. This one.'

'But it's just rumour, isn't it? From the mouth of a criminal. Well, we'll do what we can.'

The voice at the other end of the line had been decidedly unenthusiastic. Which was why Maubourg had taken it upon himself to pay a personal visit.

It was against proper protocol, of course. He should have left the matter entirely in the hands of his brother officers at Versailles.

Another reason for keeping this visit as discreet as possible.

Madame had leapt to the right conclusion, in her admirable, irritating way.

'And I have had no warning at all from the Versailles police, so you've come yourself. Well, thank you, I'm in your debt.'

She might have said more, for she was speaking with some feeling, but Florence came rushing into the room.

'Daniel says it's all ready - oh, Monsieur Maubourg! Hallo!'

At dinner - cress soup, fillet and salad, strawberries - Maubourg and Florence exchanged news of schools - his daughter's lycée in Cannes, her little school in Versailles - and after dinner she darted off to her room to watch a ballet video. 'I love the dancers, you know! I want to be one.'

She twirled off. Cecile was laughing. 'She's a graceful child - much more than I was at her age. She might make a dancer yet.'

'They all seem so thin,' ventured Maubourg.

'Yes - like models. And it's a very short career. What is Rachelle doing?'

He told them about her plans to study philosophy, and they talked about universities and careers for a while, till he said he really had to catch the next train back to Paris, and left for the Rive Gauche station.

Meanwhile, somewhere in the brilliant light of the south coast, a blind was pulled down to shut out the sun. Word was out that White Boy wanted an address. Anywhere in France, anywhere abroad.

So a computer screen flashed into life in the darkened room, and the engines of the Internet searched away. Magistrates can't use pseudonyms, and it wasn't even necessary to consult one of the official lists.

There were a number of responses to the search enquiry, but they weren't really needed. There is virtually no anonymity with the Internet. Almost anyone in the world can be traced, anyone who can't disappear, any professional person. The first result was a report of a local case in Les Nouvelles de Versailles: a woman magistrate had ordered a number of teddy bears destroyed. It was the kind of case that catches the eye of the editor of the local paper.

The man tapping away at the keyboard gave a long sigh of satisfaction.

Chapter Eighteen

There was a stream running through the grass and the child could see, lying with her chin pressed to the ground, a new world. A river, with great cliffs arising, a tangled forest hanging over the banks. Something she did not understand lay in the air over the water, like the shadows moving on its surface, as she lay on the ground and tried to understand what the starlings were saying.

Her sister had told her once there was a whole tree growing under a pool, its topmost branches floating on the surface of the water. She dreamed of it sometimes as she drifted off to sleep in the big grey house.

Her mother was coming towards her, telling her to get up off the grass.

'Don't you want to go and help William in the garden?'

In the mornings, William washed his red neck under the pump out in the yard. When he dug the kitchen garden, she watched for the worms and pulled them out with her fingers and put them in a bundle, all tangled up. When William finished, he put the spade against the wall and picked up the worms like strings. He held the bundle of them in one hand. Then he went to the chicken house and pulled the live worms into bits, throwing them to the chickens to gobble up. The wriggling pieces disappeared into the red beaks. All the bright little brown eyes stared greedily round for more, peering at her sideways.

That had been such a long time ago, thought the grown woman, remembering it many years later. It scarcely seemed possible now, that childish existence and yet sometimes the intensities it had revealed to her, those inner moments, returned. She hid them, ever since her brother had advised her that the world would not understand her vision of the Bishop's Birds, yet her reading secretly encouraged her and could be openly discussed. The study of the works of the prophets could surely not be accounted an indulgence or an extravagance, either in her private thoughts or in the feelings it might inspire in her students. There was no question that it might lead any young mind astray.

Waiting for them to come in for this morning's lecture, she bent her head down to the thin gilt-edged India-paper pages.

'And I turned to see the voice that spake with me. And being turned I saw seven gold candlesticks.' She saw them, in her mind's eye: they floated in the dim room, glittering, tipped with flames, miraculously aloft.

She forgot where she was, almost, and read on, her face avid, as if hungry for what she read.

'And immediately I was in the spirit: and behold, a throne was set in heaven, and one sat on the throne ... and there was a rainbow round about the throne in sight like unto an emerald ... and before the throne there was a sea of glass like crystal: and in the midst of the throne, and round about the throne, were four beasts full of eyes before and behind -'

Yes, she saw them! Great gilded creatures, with sleek backs, rippling manes and ruby eyes, and before them stretching away for ever, into the far distance, the great glimmering stretch of glass, dazzling, reflecting - Annie Moberly felt herself slipping away and into another world: that was the wonderful thing about religion, these intense feelings of happiness and joy, the sense of escaping, that was the reward of the faithful, surely. Robert, her brother, had never encouraged these feelings, it was true, but she had ceased to mention them to Robert long ago. She longed for someone with whom to share her inner life, a true companion spirit.

Something was breaking into her thoughts. She brought herself back to the world of reality, hearing the peal of the doorbell, and the maid's footsteps as she went to the door to let in the first of the girls, for these study sessions were held in Miss Moberly's own home. They mostly arrived in small groups, falling silent as they entered, and filed into her sitting-room.

There was a little late sun coming through the stained glass in the front door of the house in North Oxford. The hallway was dark, nevertheless, but the room beyond it was warmly furnished with Persian carpets and watercolours, patches glowing damson and navy in the dim gaslight. Through the French windows, the students could see the wet shrubbery beyond, the dark green branches of Solomon's Seal and the frail twigs of the orange-blossom, as they waited for the commencement of the Principal's private lecture in her house in Norham Road. Abruptly, putting back her head, her dark eyes staring intently around, Miss Moberly launched straight into her theme. This term all her lectures would be on the Book of Revelations.

The young women were already settled in a circle around their hostess's chair. Miss Moberly was sitting bolt upright, as usual. She seemed to be waiting for something - divine inspiration, no doubt, or maybe possession would be a better word. It was the fascination of watching a human being in the full grip of something beyond herself, said one of the most promising students, when she talked about Miss Moberly to a friend, many years later. 'That's why I went. Not for what she said. Just for this extraordinary drama she created. It was like something from another age, the era of evangelical preachers, perhaps. She struck me as someone possessed.'

Chapter Nineteen

'There's a woman asking to see you. Mademoiselle Élise Barrau. I've spoken to her but she insists on seeing you.'

Jean-Claude Guillemet, Cecile's clerk, pulled the knot of his tie slightly to one side, reading the name carefully from a piece of paper. Cecile longed to stare fixedly at a point just below his Adam's apple and exclaim, 'It's not straight!' but desisted. It would be too cruel.

'Did you ask what she wanted?'

'Of course, madame.'

Cecile bit her lip. Why did almost anything she said to Jean-Claude get taken as a reproof when she was always so careful? ... well, perhaps it was because she tried to be so careful, that mixture of being extra-correct and extra-sensitive was so difficult to deal with. They had to be a team, the *juge d'instruction* and her clerk, and she had managed to create that eventually with Lenoir, the bespectacled curly-headed *greffier* who had served her well in Cannes.

Jean-Claude was telling her some more about the woman who wanted to see her.

'I recommended, *madame le juge*, that she should go to the police, or to the Prosecutor's Office, with the information.'

Tried to fob her off, translated Cecile to herself. 'What information?'

'She says a friend of hers has disappeared.'

'Well, it really is a matter for the police, then.'

'She's sitting outside. Said she had seen an article about you in *France-Soir* and she had made up her mind you could help her. She doesn't seem to understand what the correct procedure is. I told her you would probably be unable to speak to her.'

'Ah, well, I suppose I can. I'm a public servant after all, but it'll just be a question of sending her on through the proper channels.' Jean-Claude looked as though he felt betrayed, so she added, 'Only for five minutes, of course. I'm sure I shan't be able to add anything to what you said.'

'Shall I send her in now?'

'Yes, do.'

The woman who walked through the door of Cecile's inner sanctum, the office which lay beyond Jean-Claude's immaculately tidy domain, was probably in her mid-thirties, with short permed blonde hair and a tartan ra-ra skirt. No wonder Jean-Claude had looked so disapproving!

But she's having a good look at everything, thought Cecile, as she motioned to Élise Barrau to take a seat. Doesn't miss much, in spite of the dolly-bird image.

'Are you Madame Galant, the instructing judge?'

'Yes, I am. What can I do for you?'

'It was that thing about toys.'

'Toys?' It took Cecile a few moments to work this one out.

'Yes, it was in the paper. You banned the toys. The bears.'

'Oh, yes, that's right, I did.'

Perhaps this woman was going to make a complaint about the judgement, though she didn't exactly look as though she was in the toy business.

'That's why I wanted to come to you. You get things done, that's what it means.'

'Well, I take that as a compliment, thank you,' said Cecile, recalling the details of the case. The autopsy on a baby had revealed traces of plastic foam in the lungs and air-passages. The foam was identical with that used to stuff a Korean-manufactured toy bear with nylon fur. The stitching on the toy, and indeed on the whole batch remaining in the shop where it had been bought, was defective and the stuff had got into the tiny mouth. 'Of course, the baby chewed it!' Cecile said, when presented with the shop-keeper's protests. 'That's what babies do. What do you expect?'

Cecile had ordered the entire stock of bears to be destroyed. There had been some humorous comments on it - 'The Lady Bear-Killer' and so forth - but there had also been an adverse police comment emanating from a very senior level: the investigation and destruction, it had been implied, were below the interest of the magistracy - even a waste of police time. 'Another accident is very unlikely - besides, they are just cheap toys.'

It had been Colas, the Commissaire or Chief Inspector, irritated because his men, the *police judiciaire*, the national force for dealing with serious matters, had been used to trace the origins of the foam, whereas a simple investigation by the uniformed squad of the *gendarmerie* might have sufficed. Cecile had looked up from her desk at his angry face.

'What it is it? That your men were expected to take the death of a baby seriously? Or that the mother was poor?'

Cecile had spoken with more feeling in her voice than she usually allowed herself, fuelled with a white-hot anger that suddenly seemed to burn its way through her, and her words were like a whip-lash of contempt. Colas had looked shocked, stunned, and the rebuke had been a public one, for there were clerks and secretaries around them.

The exchange, of course, had not been reported in the papers, though the decision to confiscate the bears had made headlines, but it had undoubtedly circulated around the Palais de Justice and outside into the community. The town of Versailles, under the huge waves of tourists that pounded and receded with every passing day, was actually a small place, full of gossip.

Cecile looked with interest at the woman before her. 'You have children, perhaps?'

'No - no, it's not about that. I just saw your name, that's all, so I knew there was someone to ask for.'

'And?'

'There's someone missing. A friend of mine. She was going to have a baby - but that's nothing to do with it, really.'

'It's a matter for the police, if she's missing. Have you reported it?'

'Yes - but they didn't take a blind bit of notice. The bloke I spoke to didn't even write it down. Said she's probably just been picked up by some rich tourist and gone off with him, and when I said she wasn't like that, he said, well, you may not be darling, but you'd be surprised at how many are.'

'Tell me briefly what happened.'

Cecile made one or two notes as the woman spoke. Then she said, 'We have a phone number for you? Good. Someone will contact you, I promise you that.'

The sharp grey eyes under their thin little brows looked suspiciously at Cecile. 'Well, there's nothing more I can do for her. I promised her once, and I've done my best.'

She picked up her red leather bag with American-style studs, and walked out.

'I don't know whether there's anything in it,' Cecile said to Daniel that evening. 'It's more important than that damned Vouet shoplifting business, anyway.'

'Mmm,' said Daniel, absent-mindedly. She walked across the room and peered at the computer screen, where improbably glossy and perfect race-horses thundered down an immaculate course. Daniel had been working for some time on programmes for simulating racing odds, an activity which paid considerably better than formal teaching of computer studies.

'Which one should I put some money on?' she said.

'Me! Good news, darling - I had a call this afternoon. There's a cable company who want a system for cyber-racing. You subscribe to a channel and the winners are determined by programming.'

'And they want your programmes? That's wonderful!'

'Yes, but look at this screen carefully. What do you think about these horses?'

Cecile peered at the shiny flanks, the sharp-cut ears. 'Well, I don't know much about the beasts, but they *look* like computer images, if you know what I mean. Not like real horses. There are no flecks of foam, no shying away to the side.'

'Exactly. They're too perfect. If this is network is to be a substitute for a real day out at the races, it's got to give the punters a bit more atmosphere - the kind of thing you would get if you were actually there. The horses behaving unpredictably, for example. Now, the one thing I do know about race-horses is that they're very sensitive, unpredictable creatures - and they're all individuals. I've got to introduce more random elements here. And on the course, too. The turf should be torn up here and there.'

'And you want a few dubious-looking characters hanging round, in old tweeds and red scarves.'

'Yes, perfect! You'd practically be able to smell the horse-shit. Seriously, this should mean a good contract for us.'

He turned round and looked up at her, twirled his chair round and put his arms round her waist.

Cecile laughed. 'Maybe we can have that expensive trip to Antarctica after all! Florence would love to see real penguins. I must admit, I adore them, too.'

'Yeah! Got to work harder on the horses, though. They're such damned nervous creatures.'

Much later, when Audran was desperately casting around in what seemed a fruitless search, Cecile was to recall this conversation, though it didn't appear to be of much significance at the time.

Chapter Twenty

Cecile took the call from the Public Prosecutor's Office: the first of the day. She had wanted to walk to the Palais de Justice and her new office, but Daniel had persuaded her not to. 'You would be more vulnerable that way.'

'I can't give up all my freedoms just because of some thug in a prison in Lyons!'

But it was bravado, and she gave in without argument, sensing for the first time not only the dreadful fear that something might happen to Florence, but another terror: that her daughter might be deprived of her mother's love and protection. 'Louis would make sure she is brought up properly,' she thought, 'but does he love her? What will he teach her? To be like them - his family, clinging to what they own? He wouldn't let Daniel have much to do with her, that's certain.'

She was still thinking about her first husband and his pompous legalities when she picked up her phone. The *greffier* was already on a line in his own office next door.

'But surely it's a straightforward case - and quite a petty one!' she was saying, as Jean-Claude came into her office, after putting his head round the door with an enquiring look, and receiving a nod.

'Nevertheless, we have thought it right to refer this matter to you,' came the response.

'Isn't the evidence clear enough - surely it would warrant a prosecution without reference to a *juge d'instruction*?'

'The matter is contested. It will probably be contested to the highest level of appeal possible.'

'But it's just an ordinary case of theft!'

Cases were normally only referred to a juge d'instruction if a more serious crime appeared to have been committed.

'We're sending the papers up straight away.'

'So urgently?'

'Oui, madame le juge. The name on the dossier is Vouet. The Marquis de Vouet.'

Later, at home, she released her anger, letting her feelings out to Daniel. 'Damn it, my case-list is unending - heroin pushers, child-abusers - really damaging stuff - damaging to society, I mean. I can barely get through the really serious dossiers - and when it comes to questioning witnesses, we're under such pressure I'm always afraid I've missed something. And now, just because it's some blue-blooded aristocrat on a charge of shoplifting, I have to handle that as well! His family is very well-connected round here, it seems, especially with the head of the Prosecutor's Office. That's what Guillemet tells me, anyway.'

'Did the old fellow do it? The theft?'

'Oh, there doesn't seem to be any doubt about that, though I suppose they want me to decide that it shouldn't go forward for prosecution. But I can't ignore the evidence. He walked into a department store and put a mirror, of all things, under his coat - then walked out. The store detective caught him on the pavement, and so did the security cameras. But he's pleading not guilty!'

Daniel was thoughtful as he twirled on his steel-tubed work-chair. He didn't answer immediately, but then commented, 'Seems an odd sort of thing to steal. Why a mirror?'

But Cecile's mind was moving on. 'I've worked all my life - struggled up and out of that tower-block in Marseilles - studying at night, fighting to get through magistrate's college. And how do I end up? Pandering to this ridiculous snobbery.'

He came over and put his arm round the back of her chair. 'Darling, it's ironic, isn't it? Here's our radical of the family ending up at Versailles. It has its funny side, you must admit.'

In spite of herself, Cecile relaxed and laughed with him. ' Oh, let's not make heavy weather of it. It's a minor irritation, that's all. My old Marquis will be subject to exactly the same treatment as any other citizen, in the end. Anyway, it'll be a first offence, I expect, so he'll get off quite lightly when it comes to trial.'

Chapter Twenty-one

The beam of the torch picked out the crumbling soft red brickwork.

'These old places!' he said. 'Goes back a long way, this one. All the way to the Revolution, I should think. We did that at school.'

Marie looked at his face, deeply shadowed in the small circle of light. The strong features that had made her think his face was so handsome seemed suddenly distorted. His nose and mouth appeared huge, his cheeks cavernous. She turned her head away.

'Yeah, think of that!'

He suddenly chopped the side of his hand lightly across the back of her neck, and laughed.

'Chopped their head off with the guillotine. And held them up by the hair. God, imagine the blood spurting everywhere. Must have been rivers of it! All the veins and stuff sticking out.'

She felt sick.

'Wonder if the eyes rolled? Must have, as they were dying. Wonder if they went on rolling? Right back up into the head, like this.'

He reached out a hand to her chin, turned her face towards his and made a grimace, the pupils turning back under his lids, the eyes like blind marbles. She tried not to jerk her head away but could not help it, and he let her go, as though he had his satisfaction in the moment through watching her reactions.

'Don't like it, do you? Must have happened, though. With them heads. All lying in a basket, where they threw them. Still twitching.'

'Shut up, Toni, please.'

He said to her suddenly, 'Did you tell anyone?'

'Tell them what?'

'That I had this place. This is my secret place. Just me and you - our hiding-place.'

'No, how could I? You never even said where it was or anything.'

He seemed to relax and was gentle with her for a while, but she remembered Élise, and wondered if she had said anything that might have given something about the secret hiding-place away. Thinking about it, she was relieved that she hadn't, couldn't, have done so. Toni would have been furious with her.

Later on, he dragged the old mattresses down from the attic and called to her to come.

'Toni, what're you doing?'

'We're going to sleep down in the cellar!'

Marie, who had been feeling more relaxed, grew tense. 'Oh, no, Toni, you're joking. I couldn't!' Her voice was shaking, frightened at the thought. 'Toni, there'll be rats and all - please not!'

He was laughing at her, enjoying her terror. 'Come on down.'

'Toni, you're just doing this to frighten me.'

'All right, go and get the whisky. I need a drink, anyway. Bring it down to me.'

Perhaps she could manage that, she thought.

That had been at the start of the night.

Later, in the darkness, Marie tried to stretch her throbbing legs. There was a crack of light from above, but the space was so tiny. It had stunk in her nostrils at first, but now she could no longer smell it. The earth floor was cold beneath her, but she no longer felt a wet flow. She had stopped bleeding, she thought, fearing to move, remembering the great spasms of pain that had doubled her up, had her screaming.

'Toni, stop, stop!'

Perhaps he hadn't meant to do this. When it started, when he slapped her because she wanted to go back up the cellar steps, it was almost casual. She didn't think he really meant to hurt her, even. But then the blood had run down from her cut lip and she stayed there, on the old bed.

'We're staying down here, I told you!'

Marie was frightened, but not yet so much that she obeyed him. She had encountered rough men before and her motto was never to let them walk over her. Besides, she didn't think seriously he would hit her again. That time before, he had seemed so contrite afterwards, almost whimpering, touching her cheek. 'Poor Marie, my poor little Marie'.

But he wasn't like that now. It was almost as if talking about those horrible things, the guillotine, the heads, had started him off on something else. She put her hand to her mouth and it came away with blood on it. She didn't really understand what was happening, wasn't yet cowed.

'Let me go, you bastard!'

His face changed as he looked at her. Maybe it was what she said, or the sight of the blood on her mouth, maybe it was her refusal to do what he wanted, but the muscles of his face seemed to contort into a look she had never seen before on any human face.

He drew back his fist and gave her a punch so powerful she rolled sideways.

'Get up, bitch!'

'Toni!'

She spoke his name as if she were trying to recall someone else.

He stared at her as if he had never seen her before in his life, the pupils of his eyes enormous, and then he hit her again, and now she couldn't get up, tried to cling to the wall for support. 'He's gone crazy,' she thought, and her knees gave way. She fell heavily on the floor, and he began kicking at her, as if she were a piece of inert rubbish on which he could vent some terrible rage. She passed out.

But when he saw it, saw the blood pouring from between her legs, he had grabbed hold of her and pushed her down on one of the mattresses. She screamed, but no one could have heard her anyway, because the house was so isolated, and once she was in the cellar it was like being in a dungeon underground.

'I don't want the bloody thing! I never wanted it, don't you understand!'

Too late, she had realised how far gone he was, how damaged, that some kind of special obscene fear lay behind his shouts and violence.

And he would not, perhaps he could not, relent or help her once he had realised what was happening. The contractions that had expelled the bloody foetus on to the cellar floor had horrified, disgusted him, urged him into even more hatred.

She passed out, and when she came to the door at the top of the steps was open and he was outlined as a black shape, the line of his head horribly familiar against the light. She had never feared it before.

He came slowly down the cellar steps.

She looked up, but found she was unable to rise to her feet. Her legs were too weak: at most she seemed able to shift her arms and push herself up on the makeshift bed.

She saw the pathetic thing lying there between her legs, a few inches long only, curled up, as if its mother might still protect it, a tiny thing not like a human yet, with a gross head, barely recognisable for what it was, in an enveloping bloody membrane.

She heard a strange sound, and saw that he was vomiting. He stumbled up the steps, and a few minutes later he came back.

He dropped something down into the cellar with a clanging noise that echoed explosively in the confined space, off the old bricks, a sound like a drum-roll. She recognised it: a metal pail for washing the floors.

He threw some old cloths down after it.

'Get rid of it. In there.'

He slammed the door again.

She thought she couldn't bear it at first, putting her head in her hands and shrieking with pain and despair. But in the dim light, she eventually did what she could, tenderly, cleaning it, like a mother animal in a cage.

Chapter Twenty-two

Cecile was on the phone to the Public Prosecutor's office. Any official investigation to be undertaken by a *juge d'instruction* had to begin there: it was for the prosecutor to refer a matter to the judge. If the judge found evidence that a crime had been committed, then the wheel came full circle, and the case went back to the prosecution to be taken to court.

Now Cecile wanted to do things the other way round: she wanted to initiate a matter, to interest the Prosecutor's Office in the case of this missing woman, Marie Calvert, reported by her friend, Élise Barrau. But the police had not been interested, and neither was the Prosecutor's Office.

'Yes, well we appreciate the information, of course, but is there any reason to suspect a crime - or any infringement of the law?'

'No, but I want someone to take a statement from this Mademoiselle Barrau.'

'Madame, do you realise how busy we all are this week - another Summit Conference, the security arrangements ...'

'Yes, more visiting Heads of State.'

Off with their Heads! There's always some potentate at Versailles, even now, Cecile thought to herself, being entertained almost as lavishly as King Louis, with the poor still at the gates. What did we have a Revolution for?

But she kept these thoughts to herself. She wanted to get something done, and appearing to the Prosecutor's Office as a burning brand of republican zeal would not achieve results at the moment. She put the phone down after a polite phrase or two.

That evening, after the day's case-load had been finally closed, she sat back for a few minutes drinking a last cup of lukewarm coffee. She longed simply to go home, to forget the whole day, but she had made a promise and, it seemed, she would have to keep it herself. 'Justice - it's finally down to me, in a way,' she thought with a laugh. 'Because I seem to be the only person in the world who cares about it.'

'Do you want to see the English woman again?' Her clerk had put his head round the door. 'Her boyfriend's coming from England to collect her - she's just telephoned to ask if it's all right to leave France.'

Cecile rubbed the back of her neck, easing the stiffness a little. 'I don't think there's any point in keeping her here. Perhaps she's got a psychological problem if she's fantasized the whole thing. But I want to see him - the boyfriend.'

'OK, I'll make a note to keep us informed. Goodnight, *madame le juge.*'

'Goodnight.'

Sometime, when she got to know him better, they might go and have a drink together, or she could ask him round to meet Daniel. Cecile was deeply conscious of the need to make human contact with her staff, resolved frequently to do so, yet seemed always to be finding that other demands got in the way of the friendly word, the casual invitation.

There was something tonight that she wanted to do in the office before she left, because she didn't want Florence to hear it, and she didn't like having secrets from the child at home.

'*Maman*?'

'Oh, darling, how are you?'

Babette's voice came down the line from Marseilles, a warm, harsh southern voice, and at the sound Cecile felt suddenly and desperately homesick. 'What am I doing here among all these rich powerful people?' she thought. 'What use am I here? That's where I belong!'

'I've been sitting on the balcony, Cecile - it's a real hot night. I can see all the lights of the port.'

Cecile thought of the sprawling, rough southern city spread out before her mother's little eyrie up on the sixth floor, the narrow streets, the scents of garlic and jasmine and rubbish-dumps that the whole place exhaled at night.

'Can I speak to my little cream-cake?'

'*Maman*, Flo isn't here. I'm not phoning from home, I'm in the office still. I wanted to ask you something - will you have Flo to stay?'

'*Chérie*, how could you doubt it for a moment. You know how much I adore her! But what will Louis say?'

'I don't care about Louis and his respectable family. I want her to be with you.'

'Why, what's the matter? I can hear there's something wrong.'

'Yes, but don't be worried, *Maman*. It's just that I've had a tip-off, that's all.'

Her mother's voice was suddenly tense with anxiety.

'What about?'

'Well, there was a man, called White Boy - '

'Yes, I remember. The gangster, the case in Cannes, last year. But he's in prison.'

'He's still a very powerful man. Lots of contacts.'

There was a silence, then her mother understood.

'So - there are threats?'

'Maubourg thinks so.'

'The policeman you worked with?'

'Yes, he's warned me.'

'Listen, you should all come here. Right away - I can squeeze you all in. You'd be quite safe here - no one has ever heard of me!'

'No, we've got to stay here, Daniel and I. We've got our work.'

'Daniel, yes - but you? What about Flo and me - don't we need you?'

'*Maman*, I have a job to do here.'

'Oh, Cecile, you make me despair, you really do. Well, of course, I'll have Flo, whenever you like - you know how I'm crazy about her! When will you bring her?'

'At the weekend? Probably on Saturday?'

'All right, darling. I'll be in, don't worry.'

At home they had a light supper, omelette with herbs and a glass of wine. Later that evening, after Florence had gone to bed and they were relaxing in the garden, Daniel said, 'Louis won't like it, I suppose.'

'Our child staying with my mother, who hasn't two pennies to rub together, when she could go to his parents in their big farmhouse? That's exactly the kind of thinking I don't want Flo to grow up with.'

'I know, darling. And you're absolutely right.'

But all the same, Louis might have some arguments on his side, she thought. After all, my brother, Guillaume, got into the drugs scene as a teenager, and got killed through it. Wasn't that evidence that Babette was a totally unsuitable person to have the care of her granddaughter, Florence? She hadn't been able to keep her own son out of trouble. It was easy enough to imagine Louis, who seemed to have been born as a miniature lawyer, putting forward all these arguments that would sound so reasonable.

Except that there were only two people in the world Cecile trusted absolutely, and Babette was one of them.

The other one got up from his chair and put his hand on her arm. 'Come on, darling, stop worrying,' he said.

'Daniel, you've read my mind, as usual!' And she laughed as they went indoors.

Chapter Twenty-three

The two British people, Marina and her boyfriend, Luke, were waiting in the outer office the following afternoon.

'I'd like to see them separately. The girl first.'

She looked subdued, worried, as she came in and perched on the edge of a chair.

'I'm allowing you to go back home to Britain, but please understand that this is subject to any further investigation.'

'Thank you, madame.'

The girl was pleating the edge of her scarf nervously, but the relief was obvious in her face.

'There's one thing I want to ask you - what caused that scar on the side of your head.'

She put her hand up suddenly, as if to hide the angry red mark automatically, then drew it back and dropped her arm, seemingly realising the action was pointless.

'I was in an accident - a road accident, about three months ago. At Woodstock, near Oxford. I was lucky - just had concussion and scalp injuries.'

Cecile felt ashamed. There had been no need to embarrass the girl, after all. But the medical report might have some bearing on her state of her mind now. She made a note on the file.

'Where were you treated for these injuries, mademoiselle?'

'At the John Radcliffe Hospital, in Oxford.'

'And the name of your doctor?'

Marina looked stubborn.

'Do you really need that information?'

'We may. It would be easy enough for us to find out.'

'You want to bring the doctors into this - you think I'm mad? I did see it, you know, in the grounds whatever they say - I saw that man being killed.'

Cecile leaned forward and said very quietly,

'But nothing has been found. No body, no trace of a crime. So inevitably, you must see, for you are an intelligent young woman, that will put the focus on to you.'

Marina sighed slowly, and stared with bewildered eyes, but she must have taken the point. Rather reluctantly, Cecile thought, she gave the name and address of a doctors' practice in Woodstock, Oxfordshire. 'That is near to where you live, mademoiselle?'

'Yes - look, can't I go? - I want to get away as soon as I can. If you won't believe me, there's no point in trying to say anything, is there?'

'Perhaps not. Ask Mr. Elmer to come in, please.'

'Why do you want to see him? What's he got to do with it?'

'I always like to follow up all aspects, mademoiselle.'

There was no arguing with her voice.

A few minutes later the translator Cecile had requested arrived, and took his seat at the table.

Luke Elmer sat up. Jean-Claude asked for his personal details - passport number, full name, Luke Aylward Elmer, address the same as Marina's in Woodstock, Oxfordshire, United Kingdom. How long had he known Miss Cassatt? Three years, since she had finished undergraduate studies and started post-graduate work. He had a job in local government and worked in the finance department of Oxfordshire County Council.

This information all duly translated and noted, he didn't wait for any questions from Cecile, who had been observing him as the clerk took down the information. He turned towards her straight away and lowered his voice. She wasn't sure why. He looked like the sort of young man used to charming women without too much trouble, but she didn't want to judge him too quickly. There would be differences in culture, in language, that might make her assessments untrustworthy.

All the same, she thought, as he turned his dark blue eyes towards her and smiled, creating charming dimples beside his mouth, all the same, there's a lot to be said for instinct.

'I think there's something I should tell you. About Marina's accident and how she got the scar on her head.'

Cecile said nothing. 'Let him talk,' she thought. 'I'll learn more about him like that.'

She gave a small, enquiring smile.

'She ran out into the road, you see?'

'The accident was her fault, is that what you are saying?'

'Not just that - something else.'

The interpreter shuffled, as if he sensed something was coming, something that would require more of him than a mere recital of facts.

'She ran out of the grounds of the Palace.'

They were all confused for the moment.

'But this was in England - not at Versailles,' said Cecile.

'No, not Versailles! Though perhaps it's the nearest thing we've got to it in Britain. Blenheim Palace, near Woodstock. Huge, eighteenth-century place - '

'Yes, I've heard of it.'

'You see, she ran screaming out into the road ... because ... because she said-'

Cecile thought this young man had a fine talent for suspense. But she prompted him, as he evidently wished.

'Yes? What did she say?'

'That she had seen -' Even he seemed abashed, looked down at the surface of the table. 'A woman being killed. A woman in a long dress. Marina said she had witnessed a murder.'

Cecile knew there was more.

'And?'

He looked up and across the desk at her, with his eyes staring straight across, directly into hers. 'Yes, good at body language, he knows how attractive he is to women,' flitted across Cecile's mind, even as she prepared herself for the next sentence, the vital thing that this young master of drama had built up so carefully. She could hear that Jean-Claude had stopped typing, sensed that he was poised to take down the next utterance.

'There was no murder.'

It was almost as if a sigh, of relief or astonishment it wasn't clear, emerged softly from his hearers. They waited for him to say something more, and he obliged.

'They never found a body.'

Chapter Twenty-four

Élise looked extremely surprised, as well she might be, to see the woman from the judge's office, ringing at the door at seven o'clock in the evening. An unlikely car for an official sort of person, a silver Alfa-Romeo was parked at the kerb.

'Come in, madame ... I'm sorry, I wasn't expecting anyone to call round.'

'No, and I'm sorry to intrude on you. But I thought we needed to talk some more about your missing friend and my appointments book is full for the rest of the week.'

Cecile thought this would serve: it was, after all, perfectly true. No need to underline the fact that the police appeared to be totally uninterested in investigating the disappearance of Marie.

They moved into the dark little room, and Élise swept a pair of tights off a chair with faded Turkish-style blue and red upholstery. She herself perched on the bed as her visitor sat down. Élise seemed suspicious at first, but her mind apparently eased after a minute or two: Cecile was careful not to look round the room, wasn't peering about in a snooping sort of way. She remembered how Babette had hated the social workers who came to their flat about Guillaume, poking their noses into everything. 'Poor people seem to have no privacy,' Babette had said, indignantly, once.

Élise's room was hot and damp, and through a door into a tiny kitchen Cecile saw a washing-machine churning away, and clothes hanging over an ironing-board. The sickly sweet smell of washing-powder filled the room.

'This is just an informal visit,' began Cecile, 'but I wanted to get some more details.'

Élise gave what details she could of Marie's family in Paris and Cecile jotted them down. 'But she hadn't seen anything of them for ages - they really didn't like him. At first, just after she met him, she used to go back to see them, but then - '

'Then?'

Élise got up without answering immediately. She walked over to the mirror, brushed her hand through her short blonde hair and contemplated her face for a moment. Cecile sensed that she was wondering what to say, whether to give away a confidence, perhaps, asking herself what sort of a person she, Élise, really was, seeking in the mirror for reassurance. The image reflected a small, hard face.

'Would you like a drink, madame? I've got some scotch - or maybe lemonade?'

'Scotch would be good.'

Cecile didn't like it much, but thought Élise would think her less stand-offish.

Two tumblers were produced, and some ice-cubes from a miniature ice-box in one corner.

The two women sipped and gazed at each other.

'It's good.'

'A friend gave it to me.'

Élise was in her late twenties, Cecile guessed, maybe on the game, but her skin didn't have that special pallor, her eyes looked normal, so she probably wasn't injecting, which was fairly unusual. So not in thrall to a pimp and free to speak? Yes, but there was something that frightened her, Cecile sensed it.

'Go on, tell me about when she went back home.'

'It was the last time she came round here. She told me about it. Her sister saw - they were trying on some clothes, apparently, and her sister saw these big bruises - in her ribs.'

Élise touched her own side in indication, perhaps in unconscious sympathy.

'He beat her up?'

'He'd kicked her in the ribs, she admitted it. And the sister told her not to go back to him - that she was mad if she did. Apparently the whole family were on at her - well, there isn't a father - but the rest of them, they all said to leave him.'

'And she went back?'

'Yes. They told her he must be a mad bastard - I told her too, but she took no notice. I'd thought till then he wasn't too bad, but that really made me scared for her.'

'Did he ever come here?'

'Him? No. Marie did, she came to see me once or twice a week, every week, but he didn't know about that, of course, though we just had a drink and a laugh. But he was the sort who couldn't bear her doing anything he didn't know about - wanted to rule her life completely. She changed, while she was with him, turned into someone who seemed very frightened at the time, know what I mean?'

Cecile nodded her head, taking another sip from her glass. It was heavy, good quality, Bohemian crystal, probably. Élise saw her looking, and tapped the rim of her own glass with a laugh. 'Nice, aren't they. I like decent things, but I can't get them, most of the time. That's the story of my life.' She laughed and settled back against the wall.

Cecile said, 'How long is it since you've seen her?'

'A month, now. She was pregnant, wanted to keep it. And he wasn't going to like that - I thought, anyway. Competition for him, a baby - he wanted Marie devoted to him, body and soul. One of those men, you know.'

'She hadn't told him, the last time you saw her?'

'No, but it was beginning to be pretty obvious - she was going to have to tell him soon, or he'd see for himself. He's not stupid, not the sort of man you can fool. She was going to tell him and I haven't seen her since.'

'Do you know where he lives?'

'She's not there, I'm certain. I went round there, a couple of times, when I knew he'd be in the bar. I looked through the windows and banged on the door and there was no sign of her.'

'Any chance she went back to her family after all?'

'No. I phoned the sister - they hadn't seen her for months.'

'Was there anywhere else she might be, anywhere Marie mentioned?'

'She did say something - about how he had found this old place where he used to take her, somewhere on the edge of a park, it was. Just all empty - but he liked to go there. And she thought - well she said she thought it was lovely, because there was trees all round, nothing but trees and birds. "That's fine in the summer," I said, "but think of it in the winter." But she wasn't bothered. That was the last time we talked - the last time she came round here.'

'Tell me, do you have any special cause for being worried - she might just have gone off somewhere, mightn't she, especially if he was violent?'

Élise put her glass down on the floor beside the bed.

'It was this funny thing she said to me once.'

'Yes?'

'She said, "If I went missing, would you look for me?" Almost as if she had thought about it. As if she was frightened of it. And there could have only been one reason she felt like that, couldn't there.'

Their eyes met.

Cecile set down her glass.

Chapter Twenty-five

'I think there *is* reason to believe a crime has been committed. I would recommend an investigation - this woman was linked to a very violent man.'

'Of her own choosing, it seems.'

'We don't know that her disappearance was of her own choosing.'

'He has a record?'

'Yes - I've checked. Armed robbery - he served five years, after remission. He'd already served a sentence for an attack on a man in a bar, when he was eighteen. He struck him in the face and broke his jaw.'

Colas of the *police judiciare* looked up from the dossier which Cecile had put before him. 'There's not much to go on here, *madame le juge*. He drinks regularly in this bar, the Blue Monkey, near the Chantiers station, so I'll get a man in there, ask some questions. Then there's the sister - you've got the number? OK, someone will go round and check up. But where is he living now? Did you get an address from-' he bent his head sideways, thumbing the two pages which constituted the file on Marie, 'from Élise Barrau?'

'There's a place somewhere - all Élise could tell us was that it was somewhere isolated, very old, small, out of the town. That's all Marie told her.'

Colas raised his head and stared at her. He had a plump face, yet its pink and white expanses were always creased by frowns and downward lines. It was the face that should have been given to a jolly fellow, thought Cecile, an odd visage for this deeply serious man.

'There's very little we can do without more than that.'

'Yes, I know.'

'In fact, it seems to me it's a waste of manpower. There's no suspicion of any crime.'

'Leave that to me to decide, please, Inspector!'

He was getting angry, she sensed it, and there was no point in that.

'The disappearance of a person connected with a man such as Toni Douet is suspicious in itself,' she said. 'At least, he could perhaps be traced through his known associates and locations.'

'By which you mean the Blue Monkey?'

'Thank you, Inspector. You will make sure Élise Barrau's name doesn't get out?'

'I suppose it could be dangerous for her, yes, even if nothing's happened to her friend. Nasty piece of work, this bastard. Won't do any harm to turn him over a bit.

Chapter Twenty-six

'What have we got on the list?' Jean-Claude Guillemet had come into Cecile's office, holding her list of examinations for the day.

'There's something just come in from the Parquet, madame.' This was the Public Prosecutor's Office, where Cecile's instructions originated. 'They want you to phone them urgently.'

Cecile sighed at the thought of a possible disruption to her tightly-planned morning. 'Better do it first, I suppose. Then I'll take the rest, as we planned.'

But that turned out to be impossible.

Half an hour later, she was pulling up outside a tall grey house that closely resembled the one in which she and Daniel were living. Jean-Claude was getting out of the passenger seat. 'Did you phone ahead and tell them I was going to visit the scene?' she asked.

'Yes. I spoke to a Lieutenant Audran of the gendarmerie. He's in charge.'

They mounted the short flight of steps to the entrance of one of the elegant houses that are a feature of the town of Versailles, ranged along the meticulously-planned boulevards, as carefully regimented as the architecture of the Château itself, created with the same deliberate care, so that there are long vistas of these old mansions, most now turned into apartments or offices.

But this house didn't seem to have been divided up. Passing through the heavy old doorway, Cecile noticed the furniture, antique though shabby, chairs with faded gilt legs and worn velvet. Though there were some rugs and tapestries on the walls, they looked second-rate and threadbare.

In the hallway, hanging like some great insect from a central hook that should have held a crystal chandelier, was the body of a man.

The hall floor seemed full of points of glittering light, and Cecile could not for a few moments think what was causing it. She was reminded briefly of those Indian textiles that have tiny mirrors set into bands of embroidery, flashing and reflecting, averting evil.

Then, as her eyes adjusted, she saw that the man's body was surrounded by hundreds of shards of glass, silvery, jagged. It lay in big pieces below his feet, that twisted slowly as she watched, and smaller fragments were scattered around, out to the walls. A couple of gendarmes were standing on chairs in the act of taking down the body and the glass fragments crunched audibly as the chair-legs took the weight.

'He's been dead for an hour, at least, I would think.'

The police pathologist, presumably. He was peering at the swollen face. Two medics entered with a stretcher, evidently preparatory to removing the body.

Cecile's voice cut through the hallway, through the sounds of sobbing that emanated from the next room. 'I gave no instruction to take him down.'

A tall man in uniform emerged from an inner room and Cecile repeated what she had just said, sharply asking the man's name and telling him, 'I am the *juge d'instruction*. The Prosecutor's Office has just handed this case to me, and there are only two reasons for destroying possible evidence in this fashion. One is that the man's life might still be saved, which I gather was evidently impossible when he was found, and the other is that I give you my permission.'

He was a tall, gangling man who had reddish-brown hair, quick hazel eyes and a thin face with lips that compressed tightly at her rebuke before he identified himself.

'Lieutenant Audran - *madame le juge*, the doctor has already examined the body and there is surely no reason to cause any unnecessary distress to the widow'.

There was something determined about him, something that hinted at a man who didn't concede easily. Cecile felt there was a process of squaring-up going on. Not confrontation, she wouldn't put it as dramatically as that. More the sense of someone who was assessing her, strange and discomforting. She spoke rather more sharply than she might otherwise have done.

'Have we had an identification, lieutenant?'

'Not formally. But there is no doubt that this was the Marquis de

Vouet. They still used the title, incidentally. They won't give them up, these old families.'

The pathologist, turning towards them as the stretcher with the bagged body was taken out of the hallway, added, 'And this is the old town house of the Vouets - some of the nobles had houses in the town, outside the Château.'

'How ever did they cling on here, through the Revolution?'

'Oh, they didn't. The house was ransacked, of course, and the family fled to England. But after the Revolution, when the monarchy was restored, the Vouets returned.'

Looking at the dangling rope, Cecile felt sick. Could she have anticipated this? Had there been anything in the way the man reacted to her interrogation which might have warranted an order for a psychiatric examination? Maybe she should have done it - maybe she could have saved this life. Yet at the same time, Cecile felt an access of irritation at the history lesson she had just been given, which seemed to rub in the fact that she was a mere newcomer, unused to the peculiar records of this strange little town which had clung to the skirts of royalty and still somehow found an existence as a stage for grand occasions.

The pathologist introduced himself. 'Locard - forensic examiner.'

'And what are your immediate conclusions?'

She gestured to Guillemet, who had produced a small laptop and placed it on an old table, where it sat oddly on the treacly brown wood, its green cursor winking. He began to rapidly record the pathologists's comments, tapping furiously with four or five fingers.

'All the signs are that the death was self-inflicted. The ligature appears to be a dressing-gown cord, knotted under the left ear and apart from the signs of strangulation, there are no other superficial wounds or injuries.'

The hallway was high, the hook probably twelve feet above their heads. Beneath it, a household ladder lay on its side.

'Please make a note of that.'

Guillemet's fingers moved quickly on the keypad.

Cecile looked around the hall. 'And note the fragments of mirror scattered in all directions, the largest pieces directly under the piece of rope that dangled from the hook. And please remove that piece of rope and bag it for evidence, Lieutenant.'

As he moved towards the ladder, she added, 'No, please don't move that for the moment. Perhaps you can get one from somewhere else. And of course, you'll be wearing gloves when you touch the rope.'

Audran scowled, to no effect. Cecile had seen too many scowls to be worried.

'There doesn't seem to have been a note, madame. So far, at any rate, we haven't found one. So we're still looking for a reason for suicide.'

'I think I can give you one, Lieutenant. The Marquis was to be charged with a crime. A small one, but very humiliating for one of his social standing. He was to be charged with theft.'

'With theft, madame?'

'Not attractive, is it? With shoplifting, to be precise. With the theft of a mirror.'

Chapter Twenty-seven

Florence was carefully putting some nuts out on a little table in the garden, for squirrels. The peanuts were in a big plastic bag from the supermarket.

'Do you think they'll come to our garden, *Maman*? There are lots in the park.'

'Yes, I expect they will. But I'm not sure, at this time of the year. Perhaps they'll come later on, when the autumn comes and they need to store up their food for the winter. Come on, darling let's get you into bed.'

Later on, after Flo had been tucked up, Cecile emerged from the child's bedroom and joined Daniel, looking out of the window. The garden looked dark, the leaves moving in the evening breeze. Daniel went to draw the curtains.

'No, leave them for a bit. I like looking out at the dusk.'

He moved back into the room as Cecile said, 'Let's leave the lights out for a bit.'

He looked at her with a touch of anxiety. 'You sound a bit gloomy. Were there problems at work today?'

'You are my willow,' she said, 'I learned that from a Czech friend - it means someone who will listen to all your troubles, as if you ran down to the riverside and murmured them all into the trunk of a willow-tree. Yes, I do keep thinking of that man, the suicide, the Marquis, as he made sure everyone called him.'

'Hard for you to deal with?'

'Yes. And it was hard for me to deal with myself. Was I prejudiced? These old aristos - they do seem a ridiculous class to me, people who expect bowing and scraping in the twenty-first century.'

'So what is it, exactly, that bothers you?'

He looked into her face with concern, seeing that something was troubling her deeply.

'That he was mentally ill. That he was in such an unbalanced state of mind that he was willing to commit suicide over something so stupid as the theft of a cheap mirror, and I didn't spot it, or refer him to a psychiatrist.'

Daniel put an arm around her. 'You can't blame yourself for not reading his mind!'

'I suppose not. Oh, I think I need some fresh air. Sorry, darling, I'm bad company at the moment. Too much work on my mind.'

The silver Alfa was still sitting in the drive.

'Do you want to take a drive somewhere?'

'Maybe. Will you stay with Florence - she should stay asleep, now, but there's always the chance she might wake up.'

'Yes - I've got some figures to check, anyway.'

Cecile fetched her bag and walked out to the car, automatically sliding into the driving-seat and inserting the key in the ignition, feeling a breeze moving through the soft evening air.

Leaving the driver's door open, she slipped back towards the house for her jacket, calling to Daniel as she walked back into the hallway.

'It's a bit chilly - I think I'll just get ...'

Afterwards, she was unable to analyse exactly what had happened as she said these words. At the time, she was aware of a great thumping sound that seemed at the same time to be lifting her up, and then the world seemed to blow apart.

She could barely lift up her head. That was the first sensation, then she managed to open her eyes. Everything around seemed to be white: she was in a glossy bright world that hurt her eyes. But she couldn't keep them closed: someone was standing over her and she felt fingers on her eyelids, and then a dazzling beam of light was shone into them, paining her like a sword.

Chapter Twenty-eight

'A very lucky lady,' she heard a gruff voice say. 'Looks as if there's not a lot of damage. Of course, we'll give her a brain scan. But the elementary tests for concussion are negative.'

The first sensation was an agonizing pain in her head, which receded after what seemed an infinity. The voice was saying something else, but she felt incapable of understanding a word, because of the obliterating pain. Cecile felt she must make some move, some contact, but her body seemed to be beyond her control. Her eyes opened again, nervously, involuntarily, fearing the light, yet the brain was needing to seek it.

'Draw the blinds.' There was a scraping sound, and a painful glitter subsided.

She was in a strange bed, a tubular affair, in an immaculate cell of some sort, with a window opposite. There was some movement to one side, and, she slowly turned her head a little and saw a red blip fluttering on a monitor screen. 'My heart?' she thought, and there was a remote fascination about it, as if this were all happening to someone else.

'Madame, can you hear me?'

The voice seemed very faint and distant, but she managed to murmur an assent.

There was a figure in a white coat standing at the end of the bed, she saw now, and someone else beyond, just inside the doorway. She recognised the second man, but could not remember his name and somehow it seemed important, so that she struggled up a little to look better.

'It's the policeman, madame. He'll be there all the time. You were the victim of a bomb attack - and luckily for you, the explosion seems to have been premature. We haven't found any physical damage except for bruising - you'll find that painful enough, I'm afraid, but it will fade. Please - try to keep calm, though.'

For Cecile was striving now to sit up, pulling at the bedclothes and the wires that seemed like bonds and fetters tying her to the bed. A burning pain that shot through her ribs but she continued to struggle, calling out 'Florence! Florence!' from a throat that seemed almost closing with despair.

The figure from the doorway crossed the room in one or two strides and bent over her - she realised it was Audran, who had been on duty when called to the Vouet suicide. 'It's all right - your daughter is quite safe. She wasn't anywhere near the explosion. And your husband also - calm yourself, please. He's waiting outside - I'll call him in.'

The fight went out of her. She felt almost sick with relief.

Daniel's hand was in hers and they were alone in the room.

'Cecile? Thank God!'

'Where's Flo?'

'It's all right, darling, she's safe. But she's with Louis' parents.'

'Oh, she was supposed to go to my mother.'

'I know, but Louis drove out here as soon as he heard the news of the explosion and the police wanted to get Flo away as quickly as possible. I'm sorry, my love, but it seemed the safest thing at the time.'

'Babette will be so disappointed. I'll have to ring her and explain.'

'I've already done that. She understands - it'll be all right for the moment.'

'I'll talk to her later on.'

There was something else she ought to say. What was it? Something to the police. She struggled with the memory.

'I want to speak to the police. There's something that has to be done - they have to try it, anyway.'

Daniel knew better than to try and stop her, but even he was doubtful, urging her to rest, forget work, just think about herself. She tried to sit up further in bed, but it provoked a splitting headache. She really just wanted to go to sleep, and sensed her brief flash of strength might soon be exhausted, but a nurse entered and held up a syringe.

'For the pain, madame.'

It was a relief, a numbing, relaxing escape that allowed her mind to work again. The thought of arguing with Colas seemed beyond her, but through the frosted glass door of the hospital room she recognised a narrow reddish head.

'Ask Audran to come back in.'

Audran was clutching a book now.

'Are you guarding me, Lieutenant?'

Even in her rather hazy state, she was amused by his sheepish reply, by the way the book was quickly tucked out of sight into a pocket. She followed its disappearance with her gaze.

'Yes, madame. Oh, well, you see, I am studying - the gendarmerie can take examinations as a route into the *police judiciare* now - the two forces are being rationalised.'

'Yes. I'm never sure what that word means.'

They laughed together, as did Daniel, sitting at the side of the bed, and the precious moment brought her still closer to the real world. Cecile contemplated Audran carefully.

'Good,' she said. She meant that it was especially good that he was ambitious. That was something she personally understood, sympathised with, even. But she also understood that ambitious people can be pressurised, that they have special vulnerabilities. His ambition was good for her purposes.

'Listen, Lieutenant, I think we have a case of murder.'

Briefly, she outlined the Marie Calvert case, thanking her lucky stars that her mind seemed to be lucid, in spite of the shock and the tranquillising drugs. 'That woman was beaten up by a man with a known record of brutality - yes, I know they weren't what get classed as 'domestics' - he attacked a neighbour, had a fight in a bar. But they're evidence of a violent temperament.'

'Chief Inspector Colas doesn't believe ...'

'Oh, I know. He doesn't think, that just because Toni Douet has a record of attacking men, that he might have beat up his girlfriend. I know the police reasoning there - he has no previous convictions for it, therefore he's never done it. Trouble, is, women are afraid of men like him. They don't give evidence against them.'

'No point in arguing about it,' said Audran, after a pause,

thinking, as life-support technology blipped away in the background. 'No reason to argue, come to think of it. So what do you want me to do?'

'Find out if the woman, Marie Calvert, is really missing. And if she is ... where he's dumped her body.'

'You're that certain?'

Cecile Galant had sat up in the hospital bed at that point. There were deep brown shadows under her eyes, and her fair hair looked rumpled. He had never seen madame le juge like that. Somehow, it convinced him of her seriousness.

'Not only that, Lieutenant, I know that it would advance your chances of promotion once you enter the *police judiciaire*. As I have no doubt you will, and very successfully, but you will need to make a real impression to get anywhere.'

'On Chief Inspector Colas.'

'Oh, Colas will try to keep you down. He doesn't like rivals. Just remember, there are people above him.'

Audran stared at her for a long moment, his sharp brown eyes taking in everything. He's grasped it, she thought. I've hooked him. He thinks I can go higher than Colas in the game.

She felt a surge of guilty relief at embroiling this innocently ambitious man. But, she said to herself, it will be justified by results. It must be. He wants this case. He wants to find the Calvert woman.

After Audran had left, giving brief instructions to a *gendarme* keeping guard outside her door, Daniel was close to her. 'It would do you good to get away, darling - and you have to leave Versailles for a while. They've got a twenty-four hour guard at the moment -'

She felt an immense relief at the sight of Daniel's anxious face, his fair quiff of hair, his hand warm and strong in hers as he bent over her in the hospital.

'Like the President of France,' she managed to joke.

'- but they want you to get out of the firing range, so as to speak.'

'White Boy?'

'Yes, they think he's behind it. Got word from one of Maubourg's men. Apparently he's a real bastard for revenge, White Boy.'

'I wish Flo hadn't gone to Louis' parents, though.'

But that was something that had to be worried about later. Just now, she couldn't cope with anything more. Daniel brushed her hair with his fingers.

'So - worry about that later. It's off with you, now! Compulsory vacation - the world's your oyster, more or less. All you have to do is take your pick - just where do you want to go?'

'England,' she had said, and at first he thought she was joking.

Chapter Twenty-nine

Audran walked wearily into the bureau, past the Traffic and Tourist divisions that did most of the policing of this peculiar little town, where crowds of visitors ebbed and flowed like the tides, and screeching tourist coaches sent respectable pedestrians skipping like mad toddlers.

Martine was at her desk already, tapping onto her keyboard with an irritating regularity of rhythm.

'You look grim-faced!'

He managed a laugh. 'Sorry! It's just that I haven't had any time off. Colas hasn't let up on me. What's new?'

'There's a report on the vehicle explosion last night. Technical data, what the lab boys managed to trace. The explosive was a plastic based on Pentrite, probably from the former Yugoslavia in origin. That's the preliminary report anyway.'

'Useless sods! Who wants preliminaries?'

She swivelled her chair, her pale face with its aureole of thin fluffy hair looking earnestly at him. She was wearing some soft lipstick, brownish.

'You're really in a bad mood this morning!'

'Sorry. Didn't mean to snap. Just tired - been at the hospital for hours.'

'Is she all right?'

'Yeah, basically. She'd just got out of the car to go back in the house and fetch something when it happened. Shocked, hit by the blast, bruised where she was thrown to the ground. But at least she's not all over the neighbourhood like the topping on smorgasbord.'

Martine winced and spun back to her screen.

He typed his codes into the keyboard and called up the files awaiting him, which included the lab report on explosives, fairly meaningless, but at least with a comprehensible conclusion. Madame Galant's car had yielded some information: the origin of the explosive was Eastern European, but the assembly bore the imprint of a western terrorist organisation, and was not dissimilar to that of Mafia car-bombs, such as those used against the Italian judges who had tried to strike against Cosa Nostra bosses. He said, in a conciliatory tone, to Martine, who had had anti-terrorist training, 'What do you make of the explosive analysis?'

She called up the file on her own screen. 'I think there's something familiar about this: a composition of Pentrite and T4. It was used by the Italian fascist gangs, the ones that were part organised crime, part right-wing extremists. The Magliana gang, based on Rome, for example. Wasn't Madame Galant known as a committed anti-racist? That would have been a good reason for them to help out the Riviera bunch.'

'So it points to those beautiful boys in the South. She was responsible for the death of one of them, and she got the boss put inside.'

'I heard it was a police job that killed one of them.'

'It was Maubourg who finished him off, but our Madame Galant who was determined to get them. The one who died was from Corsica, and his pals may have picked up a few tips from friendly Italian neighbours.'

He stood up and walked to the window, stretching and yawning.

Martine looked thoughtfully at him. 'Want to go out for a drink this evening?'

'Why are you changing the subject?'

'You need a break. You're jumping to conclusions, aren't you?'

He felt desperately tired, suddenly, and sick of it all. Yes, he did need a break, in fact, he needed to leave for good, before he just gave in to the inevitable. He would settle into this smug little town to become another creature resigned to its cage, no longer beating against the bars. Exhaustion was another stage along that road, another part of the process that sapped your will, made you drift along the easy course. Not trying to fight Colas in any way, abandoning any struggle for independence, easy agreement - those would be markers along his path to middle age and what passed as wisdom.

'I'll talk to Maubourg. Maybe they can help in Cannes. He warned her she was in danger - they had a tip-off down there.'

Audran got himself a cup of coffee before he picked up the phone. Martine had gone out on a call.

The rasping voice at the other end of the line betrayed no shock at the attack on Cecile Galant - in fact, the man sounded as if nothing would ever surprise him again, thought Audran.

'He was going to have a go at her sooner or later. White Boy, the *capo*. He's a vicious sort of bastard, with good contacts even though he's in maximum security. And he takes revenge seriously. I think this would be a personal thing with him.'

'So this won't be the last time, that's what you're saying?'

'She needs all the protection you can give her.'

Audran leaned back and swirled the black grains around in his cup. He knew what was coming next. It was the obvious thing.

'Can't you get SPHP on to it?' said Maubourg.

The service for the protection of VIPs was an élite national unit, consisting of about five hundred men recruited after stringent testing, designed to guard against terrorist attacks as well as threats by the stalkers and psychopaths who bedevil the lives of those in the public eye.

'No good,' said Audran.

'No good? Her life is threatened, isn't it?'

'Yes, of course, there's no doubt about that. But Chief Colas has another consideration ... he's not going to approach SPHP. '

'What the shit is this about? What consideration?'

Audran said quietly and slowly, 'SPHP is for the protection of top personalities, especially politicians. Madame Galant is not important enough. There would be no embarrassment for France as far as the international community is concerned, if an attack on her were to succeed. She's a mere *juge d'instruction*, after all.'

There was a hissing at the other end of the line, a sound Audran associated with southern voices, with teeth clenching in a temporary restraint of fury.

'That's what Colas says?'

'It was what he said, yes. His exact words.'

Chapter Thirty

The room seemed cheerful enough, with chintz curtains, and there were curious little packets on a tray beside an electric kettle.

Cecile examined a small wrapper full of powder, but decided not to indulge. There was a tea-room in the main street.

Outside, the damp greenery of Blenheim Park waved in the breeze: the guest-house windows gave directly on to the Blenheim estate. In Mrs Robertson's front first-floor room, Cecile contemplated the neat pink covers and the en-suite bathroom, and then decided to sally forth. There were other, rather grand and expensive establishments in the little town, especially old inns, offering all kinds of modern de luxe comforts. She read a menu outside one of them: lunch was Haddock on Oriental Noodles with Asparagus and Mascarpone Strudel. Dinner featured Cod on Oriental Noodles, also the aforesaid Asparagus and Mascarpone, just in case there was any left over from lunch. Cecile passed on in amazement.

Blenheim Palace: a pound for admission to the grounds, unless you were a local. As she walked through the huge black and gilded iron entrance gates and down the long drive towards a vast pile of soft smoky and buff-coloured stone that towered up in the distance, she saw the lake to her left and walked towards it, as if irresistibly drawn in by the beauty of the scene. The steep-sided lake was a steely blue and the grounds were dotted with people walking dogs: a man in an orange bobble-hat ran past Cecile, a small sheepdog or something of the sort dashing in front of him. There were feathery, spreading cedars at the water's edge, and an island, like a view taken from a painting, with cypresses and a great white bird - a heron perhaps - hunched long-legged on the miniature shore.

Rounding the lake, she saw a stone bridge of grey-gold stone, spanning across wide arches, on a straight line stretching from the great house itself up to a far-distant column, a memorial, no doubt, yet also marking the expanse of this territory, emphasizing the vast extent of it, the power of its ownership.

Cecile paused, and gazed at this perfect man-made landscape, an expanse which delighted the eye in every direction, the classical pile of the Palace itself to her left, and to her right the gleaming lake-water and its fantastical island.

Absorbed, she stayed still for a few minutes and a glossy black crow, its fat feathers iridescent in the sun, landed on the grass and stalked beside her, unafraid.

It was more beautiful there than she could have imagined. She moved on: the green freshness, the sweetness of the air, drew her further along. Nearing the bridge, she saw beneath it that there were windows set in the grey old archways, the water washing in and out of them. Drowned rooms, irresistibly romantic? Yes, it was near here that it must have happened, that Marina Cassatt had seen - what? Reality - a murder? Or fantasy, the conjuration of a sick mind possessed by an overactive imagination, one that had indulged in too much daydreaming of the past, was desperate to draw attention to itself?

Making her way down towards the lake, she sat down near the mossy green edge of the water and sighed with contentment: it seemed the first time her mind and body had relaxed since before that explosion that had spared her life, yet had nevertheless blown apart the fragile framework of her existence.

The smell of cedar drifted from the roots of a huge overspreading tree, with a great hole in its trunk that might have sheltered whole colonies of small animals through the centuries. It was warm down beside the lake, well below a road which ran along at the top of the steep slope behind her. On the water before her, the sun was so bright there were diamond arrows, sometimes angled like musical notes as they danced, dazzling the eye, a radiant burst of ripples edging across the surface as the rays of light moved across the water.

There was a sudden noise from further along the lakeside, a sound which Cecile identified after a moment or two as the angry booming of a horn. At first she thought it was a car-horn, but then she realised, absurd to believe, that it was a hunt, streaming along beside the lake towards the top of the slope. A rider on a white horse, blowing the horn, was leading the chase. Then came the hounds: one after another, they leaped over a high gate, flinging themselves at it, their bodies twisting in the air with their frantic speed, baying and yelping. The other riders were strung out around the edge of the lake, all going full tilt.

Primitive noises, only once removed from bear-baiting, thought Cecile, with shock. There was a terrible squealing and barking as the hounds reach a clump of trees, the human and animals sounds tied into a knot.

Not looking back, she got up and hurried away in the direction of the house. On the way, an old man stopped her, and politely asked if she knew what species the birds on the island were. As if nothing had happened, as if nothing had died or shrieked or been driven into a frenzy within yards of where they stood.

Cecile mustered her thoughts, declining to recognise any of the wildlife. She hurried on, looking at the landscape, trying determinedly to put the concatenations of the hunt out of her head. From the bridge, a church tower was visible in the distance: does Blenheim Palace have a chapel, as would a French château? Or do the English not do these things? Cecile did not know.

The great bulk of the house rose before her, and it seemed almost as grand as Versailles, in the drama of its setting. Back near the house, there were more people: she understood the English conversation without much difficulty: a family was talking about 'The Last Emperor'. Cecile laughed, temporarily forgetting the hunt.

There was a gateway with a magnificent coat-of-arms that led through into a great pillared courtyard, but Cecile didn't want to leave the sunshine and go into the interior of the house. That would certainly be like Versailles, she thought, great gilded eighteenth-century rooms, heavy, cocooning, the air still and unmoving.

'Lie heavy on him, earth, for he
Laid many a heavy load on thee!'

Wasn't that Vanbrugh's real epitaph? She had read it in the guidebook to Oxford.

A flag, dark blue chequered crosses and coats of arms, was flying over the gateway - the Duke's insignia, presumably, reminding the world that there had been no revolution here. Outside, there was a parked car with dogs penned in the back, barking furiously as a group of children on horseback rode nearby.

She retraced her steps. At the entrance to the grounds was another inscription, and she stood back to look at it, shading her eyes against the sun.

'This gate was built the year after the death of the most illustrious John Duke of Marlborough by order of Sarah his most beloved wife to whom he left the sole direction of the many things that remained unfinished of this fabrick.'

Good for Sarah, thought Cecile, as she deciphered the date as 1722. Bet she gave them hell!

Waiting for the bus to Oxford, she peered in a shop window, a small bow-fronted affair set in the local stone that she was growing to recognise. And to appreciate, she admitted to herself, looking at its grey and gold facets chipped with white, in the pale sunlight.

The contents of the shop-window seemed a mystery to her. 'Special offer: Men's Bed-Socks', she read on a small hand-lettered sign. What on earth were those? And there were other garments here 'pantees and vests'. 'Pantees' - that was new, she would look it up in her dictionary. There were one or two things that seemed familiar, a blue nightdress, 'brushed cotton', apparently. The look of it took her back to her childhood, for a few moments. Hadn't her grandmother worn something like that, when she came to stay with them? Cecile remembered the talcum-powdery smell of it. Her grandmother's had been faded, washed out, soft.

The bus to Oxford arrived as she was contemplating this memory. On the way the wall surrounding the Blenheim estate seemed to stretch all along the side of the road. Then it ended, and soon she saw untidy scraps of ground.

Chapter Thirty-one

In one of the tall narrow Cotswold stone houses overlooking the main street in Woodstock, Marina Cassatt turned and looked at Luke with a gesture of despair.

'She'll be here in Woodstock, and I've promised to see her. She phoned me yesterday - it's supposed to be quite informal.'

'You don't have to talk to her. You don't have to say anything at all to her. This is England - what can some French lawyer do here?'

'She isn't just a lawyer - and anyway, that's not the point.'

He came across the room.

'Listen, I don't want you to speak to her, OK? For your own sake.'

Marina turned away as Luke reached out a hand towards her. He stopped in surprise and she realised that she had never before done that to him. He seemed to soften his tone.

'Look, I'm just thinking of you, love. You were so upset in France - I don't want you to have any more - well, any more problems.'

It made things worse. 'By "problems" I suppose you mean "delusions", having everyone thinking I'm going mad,' said Marina bitterly. She reached for a coat and said, 'I'm going into Oxford - there are some things I have to look up in the library.'

'What time will you be back?'

'Oh, I suppose I'll be a few hours. I'll have something to eat in college.'

But she couldn't concentrate, somehow. She didn't even feel hungry and after leaving the Bodleian, instead of having lunch in Oxford, she caught a bus back to Woodstock with some idea of making things up. Had she been wrong, to be so sharp and quarrelsome with Luke? He had tried to look after her, she knew that, Marina told herself, as she got out her doorkey. They had a flat on the first floor, just two bedrooms, but that cost enough. Woodstock was cheaper than Oxford, but it was a very expensive place, all the same. Letting herself into the carpeted hallway, she stopped suddenly, her face turned towards the stairs. There seemed to be voices coming from their flat. It was a Saturday, so one of Luke's friends from work might have dropped in, but he hadn't mentioned that he was expecting anyone. The voices were very low, so that she could not even tell if the stranger was a man or a woman.

Her hands, which had been busily putting her doorkey away, seemed to stop of their own accord, and turn to the lock in the door, slipping it open again without any sound. Not, of course, that she was doing it deliberately. It was just that she suddenly sensed a kind of drive for self-preservation, she could put it no higher than that, an inner voice that said 'Find out!'

And the same imperative counselled her to silence, took her out of their little hallway and swept her across the road, up a short flight of steps and into the doorway of a shop that was in the convenient shadow on the other side of the street. There was a lot of traffic, buses and lorries passing all the time, so that she had difficulty in seeing who it was at first - she just saw the top edge of their front door opening, at first, over the roof of a van, and then as the vehicle slid along the street, she started to feel sick, and her world seemed to turn upside down again.

Afterwards, when she walked up the stairs and pushed open their door, Luke looked into her face, and saw it there straight away. She never had been able to hide anything from him. He went on the attack.

'You were spying on me!'

'How could you?'

'Listen, I couldn't tell you - it would all have been much worse.'

'So what am I supposed to do now? I know who it was!'

'For God's sake, don't say anything!'

She walked into the bedroom and lay down. He followed her, begging, pleading, threatening, but it was as if she had gone a long way away. Both of them felt it.

'I have to see her. I've arranged to meet her in College - she'll think it's suspicious if I don't turn up.'

'All right - oh God, Marina, I didn't want to hurt you! Please believe me.'

His eyes were looking down into hers. Perhaps he really hadn't meant to.

'How did you get involved?'

Chapter Thirty-two

St. Aldate's turned out to be a long dusty street, sloping downward towards the river. As she walked along, Cecile could see through wrought iron gates on her left to a great stretch of green. She had walked past towers and a monumental archway, part of Christ Church College, according to her guide-book, and was now bound for a low modern building nearer the river.

Inside, there was a small but very clean room, with a bench where one or two people - she noticed a young girl with rings through her cheek, and an old lady - were seated with empty expressions on their faces, and a counter. A uniformed police officer took her card, disappeared, and returned after a few minutes. He unlocked a door at the side of the counter and ushered her through. There was an angry murmur from the bench, and the old woman rose and squawked, 'I was first!'

'This lady has an appointment, Doris!'

The bench subsided. Cecile blessed English politeness.

The room she was shown into was small, bare and contained nothing but a desk, a computer terminal and a few chairs. It was remarkably like her own office in its sparse purposefulness. Slanted blinds gave onto the street and there was a constant buzz of traffic.

She waited only for a few minutes, and then a tall man appeared, extending his hand.

'Madame Galant? I'm Halley. So sorry to have kept you waiting.'

He was thin, dark-haired, with long cheekbones. A face she didn't think of as typically British, somehow, a face that hid thoughts behind it. Although perhaps they all did - even those ruddy looks she had noticed in the desk-sergeant downstairs.

'Good of you to see me, Inspector.'

He seemed surprised.

'You speak very good English!'

'Yes, I spent six months here, when I was a student, to observe your systems. Oh, not in Oxford - in London. Streatham.'

He laughed, seeming bemused by her authentic South London pronunciation of the place-name, 'Stre 'am.'

'Well, that's excellent - but you must have seen a pretty tough side of things! I understand you've come about an incident in the grounds of Blenheim Palace - at least, that's what Willis said.'

Willis had been the policeman in London, involved in the Cannes Mutilator case from the British end. He had broken the news to Charlie Cashel of his sister's death in Cannes, and followed up the activities of Charlie and his beautiful but shady girlfriend, Imelda. When Cecile had told Maubourg that she wanted to go to England to investigate the Versailles conundrum, he had contacted Willis, and got the name of a pal in the Thames Valley police division. It was this 'pal' as Willis had described him, who now sat in front of Cecile, rubbing his forefinger along a distinctly handsome chin.

'Yes. It is a very different scene, I suppose,' she answered, recalling the bustling shop-fronts of Streatham as she looked out on the charmed architecture of St. Aldate's, Oxford.

He leaned his long forearms on the desk.

He seemed a little puzzled. 'This is not an official police request - you are not connected with the police investigators?'

'No - I am a *juge d'instruction*. There is no equivalent in your system: I am appointed to be an independent investigator of serious crimes, to see if there is a case to hand over to the prosecutor. But I am neither for the defence nor for the prosecution.'

A somewhat sardonic grin appeared on his face.

'You are in search of the truth, then, madame! Yours is a difficult task, if I may say so!'

'Yes, indeed!' She appreciated his tone, but not his next remark.

'The French police presumably keep you informed of investigations?'

She had learned by experience that there was a time in such conversations when she had to make her position clear, remembering with bitter amusement the story of the woman company director preparing to interview an applicant for a job. He had walked into the room, handed her his coat, and asked her if she could rustle up a cup of coffee.

Aloud, Cecile said, 'Oh, yes, they do. Because I am in charge of their investigations, you see.'

The candidate hadn't got the job. Halley did have the grace to apologise.

'I'm sorry - I think I misunderstood the extent of your powers.'

'I control the police investigation and all research into the case where serious crime is involved - the forensic examinations, for example.'

He recovered well - if that was an exclamation of surprise, it was only just detectable.

Glancing again at the papers on his desk, he resumed, 'And you have been an examining magistrate in Marseilles and in Cannes, I understand, and are currently based in Versailles. Well, you must have experienced all of the social spectrum!'

An intelligent man, she thought, automatically assessing him, and well-informed by Willis. Was he hinting at something - the British were said to be divided over some issues in the most unexpected ways. Take fox-hunting, for instance, the spectacle she had witnessed this morning - she had read that many Conservative politicians were actually totally against it, and that there were some left-wingers, supposed to be in conflict with country land-owners, who supported it. It could well be that the forces of law and order were equally divided. But here it was regarded as a personal moral issue. Best not to mention what she had witnessed that morning. Better to think about what Marina had seen last year, in that same spot.

'We had an incident at Versailles, involving a Miss Marina Cassatt. I understand she was also responsible for an occurrence at Woodstock, near Blenheim Palace.'

'Ah, yes, Willis passed the name on to me, and I got out the file. He opened a cardboard folder in front of him, containing computer print-outs.

'Trouble was, the young lady seemed to have - I don't say she actually deliberately invented it all. But she claimed to have seen something of which we found no trace at all. '

'She said she'd seen a murder - or an attempt at one I heard that from her boyfriend, who came to France to bring her back.'

'We found nothing! Searched the site - even dragged the lake. Questioned the staff, the locals - nothing at all. She even caused an accident, running out into the road, but fortunately no one else was hurt. We were going to charge her with wasting police time at one point, but it seemed a bit of a pointless exercise - I mean, if a psychologist could give evidence that she actually believed what she had seen, that she thought she was doing her duty by coming forward - the prosecution could have just been pointless. So there were no charges against her, in the end. But what did she do in France? Willis didn't have any details of that.'

Cecile felt sad for the girl. It seemed almost like a betrayal as she answered slowly, 'She said she had seen a murder. In the grounds of the Château of Versailles.'

Halley pushed his chair back and threw his pen on the desk. He gave a sharp burst of laughter.

'And - ?'

'We found nothing.'

'So she's a pure fantasist? She goes round historic buildings, imagining things. Hysterical, attention-seeking, whatever.'

He leaned forward again and looked sharply at Cecile.

'Of course, it's helpful to know this, in case she causes any more trouble here,' he said. 'But what are you doing here, madame? We could have been informed through official channels.'

She hesitated. It might sound too slight, too feminine, damn it! But she took the plunge.

'Inspector Halley, I have interviewed many people. Our caseloads are huge - as are probably your own. But I have come to assess people very quickly and to trust my own judgement. As a good policeman does, also.'

'Yes, there's a certain amount of truth in that. We do, maybe too often, though.'

His voice was reflective.

She pressed on.

'And in this case, I felt she had actually seen something. It was the precision of her account, you see, and the fact that she didn't exaggerate anything. Yes, she thought the victim was wearing something like eighteenth-century dress, but she didn't claim to have seen Marie-Antoinette or ladies in crinolines dancing around, or anything like that. She didn't hear voices, which is always indicative of mental disturbance. And her mind seemed clear on all other topics - she was nervous, but quite rational. No delusions, except for that particular one.'

'But the matter was investigated and there was nothing to support her story?'

'No. But we have an artificial lake at Versailles, too, and before I left, I recommended to the authorities that it should be - what do you say - that it should be dragged.'

The English word had a horrible resonance, she found, suggestive of rotting things rolling in muddy nets.

'I have to be frank about this,' he said, after a moment's pause: perhaps the same thoughts were passing through his mind. 'I think she was fantasizing. You know, there's something about those places that affects people's minds, sometimes. Like those two scholarly Oxford ladies who claimed to have seen the ghosts at Versailles!'

'You've heard of them!'

'She was researching into them, wasn't she? I think it's pretty clear - it affected her brain. Blenheim is pretty close to a British version of Versailles, after all. These grand old places - they feed the imagination sometimes, I think.'

'Yes, I suppose so.'

Leaving the police station, Cecile wandered up St.Aldate's and, following the tourist track recommended in her guide-book, walked over Carfax, noisy and fume-filled, where double-decker buses swung their terrifying bulk round the cross-roads. She moved rapidly past the smell of hamburgers and the hideous conglomeration of instant take-aways that followed, and turned with relief into a wider, pedestrianised road lined with old buildings. This, her guide-book informed her, was Broad Street, famous for its bookshops as well as for its colleges. To her left, curlicued and magnificent, a majestic pair of wrought iron gates with gilded trimmings gave on to glimpses of a graceful garden lawn and lilac trees: the quintessence of Englishness, she thought with amusement.

But her mood changed rapidly as the sight of a small girl in the street dancing along, tugging on the hand of her mother, suddenly brought back the thought of Florence, and she felt the absence of her own child as a sharp physical pang. She wanted to lift her daughter up, to feel the weight of her in her arms, to smell her sweet skin. She must be growing every day, and although she phoned every evening, nothing could replace what she was missing - the mercurial, ever-changing progress of childhood.

What can I buy to take home to her, she wondered, knowing that in reality she was distracting herself, easing her own inevitable maternal guilt at leaving her child.

There was a bookshop on her right and a display of bright covers caught her eye: fantastic designs of rabbits, dancing turtles, creatures drawn with a delicate complexity that could only come from an age that predated the crudities of computer graphics.

Lewis Carroll. Hadn't he been a professor at Christ Church? Yes, only Oxford could have produced such a character, that extraordinary mixture of intense imagination and sexual repression. Surely! Inside the shop, she found every possible version of the great fable, 'Alice' in pop-up versions, in talking books, in tiny versions almost suitable for a mouse's pocket.

Buying a beautifully printed edition, with Tenniel's classic illustrations, for Florence, a thought came to her as she stepped out of the shop. She took the book out of the packet and looked through it.

Of course, Carroll hadn't written just *Alice in Wonderland*. There was *Alice through the Looking-Glass*, too. The child, gazing into the mirror, seeing her reflection, yet wondering if it might be an inhabitant of a different world. "Looking-Glass" that old evocative English word for a mirror, something you peer into, something with depth, a magical space all of its own.

Her footsteps suddenly became more purposeful, and she crossed the road.

Blackwell's Bookshop had a knowledgeable young person who directed her to a large section on myth and literature. She found what she was looking quite quickly, bought the book at the till and took it up to the coffee-room in the shop.

'Mirrors are not only functional,' she read, 'creating an illusion that the given space is bigger, if there are crowds present that it is more populous, than is actually the case. The image in the mirror has a psychological and symbolic value. It is the other self, the doppelganger.'

It suddenly came to her. Mirrors, to her, had meant the endless Galerie des Glaces at Versailles, the Sun-King's dazzling vanity that was to be reflected, enlarged, extended in the illusory kingdom on his Château walls, as well as in the painted ceiling that depicted him enthroned in majesty. But they could mean something else, as they had to Lewis Carroll, perhaps. Another soul, another self, an alternative life, perhaps.

'I didn't think about it,' and she mentally excoriated herself. 'I must talk to Colas when I get back. He'll probably say it won't make any difference, it's too late now - but it's part of the truth. Truth is the respect we owe them - the debt of the living to the dead.'

Chapter Thirty-three

'Sir, I believe we can follow up the indications given by this woman ...'

'I don't see that we have any need to believe a word she says - that *putain*!'

'She's a smalltime hooker, yes, but that doesn't mean she's not telling the truth about this.'

Audran's rational persistence was further annoying the senior man. At the bottom of it was probably Colas' well-known view, that the *gendarmerie* and the *police judiciaire* should remain separate entities, that some plodding cop on traffic duty who fancied himself as a caped crusader should not make it into the sacred ranks of agents dealing with serious crime. Audran might break through the barrier, but that did not make him welcome on the other side of it.

'Very well - but don't waste any manpower on the Marie Calvert case. You can make some enquiries yourself, but there's going to be that American state visit with a huge entourage, and I'll need everyone on board for surveillance. You have till the end of the week.'

Four days. Still, Audran reflected, he had got something - and he could have handled it worse. He could have mentioned the name of Cecile Galant, who had initiated this investigation. That would have driven his boss into a frenzy. They had already had enough trouble arranging for the water to be dragged.

The Blue Monkey tended to put off any stray tourists who ventured inside. They were afraid of the dark-haired, poorly-dressed characters who hung around outside, for a start, the flotsam and jetsam who had found their way out of the station, and who might speak strange tongues and snatch their cameras, or with amazing dexterity slip their wallets even out of their traveller's buttoned-down safety pockets. But if a tourist did unknowingly penetrate as far as the interior, there were other deterrents: the unscrubbed linoleum table-tops, a powerful odour from the pissoir at the back, a sour-faced barman, the absence of any menu or information as to the prices of drinks.

Audran, persevering through the semi-gloom, was served, if sulkily.

He showed his warrant card, but it wasn't necessary. This was a small town, in many ways.

'Toni? Never heard of him.'

'Don't give me that rubbish! You scared of him, or something?'

It hit home, Audran noted, with interest.

'So when does he come in?'

The man's features were flattened and shapeless, veterans of many combats. But he made no reply, till Audran said casually, 'You want a raid? Turning over everything in sight? Maybe smashing a few bottles when the boys get clumsy?'

That went home, too.

'Toni comes in evenings, about ten o'clock. Doesn't stay long and he hasn't been here much lately, anyway.'

'Girlfriend?

'Think she's called Marie. But maybe he's dropped her - I haven't seen her for a while. Maybe he's packed her in.'

'Did he tell you anything about her?'

'Nah. He thinks he's too good for this place, anyway. He fancies himself as a big-time boy. "Got a country house," he said, last time, laughing all over his face. "Maybe not a château but I'm on the way - oh, yes!" That's all he said, though.'

At ten o'clock that night, Audran was off-duty, lounging at home, lifting a bottle of beer. Dammit, he thought, why should I do this? Again, second night running.

Partly because it might be a means of advancement. Colas didn't like him, wouldn't give him anything automatically. He would stay at this rank all his life, as far as that bastard was concerned.

The Blue Monkey boasted its usual crowd, more light fingers inside the bar than outside on the pavement, if Audran was any judge. He pushed his way through. American tourists would never come in here, surely, not with those rolling blue clouds of smoke, those ash-trays full of Gauloises butts. The Monkey appealed to a less health-conscious clientèle.

There was a man at the bar who was better-dressed than the average punter, in a black leather jacket, supple hide, well-stitched, none of your rubbish. His back was turned towards Audran, who pushed in alongside him.

The barman swiped a hank of wet cloth across the zinc counter-top. It left a smear behind. Audran ordered a *fine*.

Pouring it, the barman inclined his head very slightly, peering cautiously out of the side of his face like a motheaten old fowl.

Audran swayed and jostled his neighbour. The response was better than he could have hoped: an instant, extreme aggression, the shoulders hunching over, the fists curling.

'What the fuck ...?'

Audran produced his card.

'Watch your tongue!'

'No one talks to me like that!' Putting up a front, chancing it.

Audran slammed his fist into the man's ribs, an upward blow, just below the heart, and as he staggered gasping, doubled up, propelled him out into the street.

'I'm looking for someone. Tell you what, let's be considerate, you sit down right here on the pavement and get your breath, and then you can give me the answer. I want to find a woman called Marie. Marie Calvert.'

Even allowing for the blow which had Audran had just delivered, the man's appearance, seen in daylight, surprised the detective. It didn't measure up to the image he had formed. The face didn't match the expensive jacket, it looked unshaven, wild-eyed, as if he had gone without sleep.

'That bitch - I threw her out. God knows where she is, probably whoring round somewhere in Paris. What the hell do you want to know about her for, anyway?'

There was probably enough to take him into the station, but Colas wouldn't hold him. Not if his card had been marked by Cecile Galant and she was safely out of the way.

'Where's this place of yours?'

Toni Douet looked at Audran, who saw that the eyes were handsome, long-lashed, in spite of their bleariness. He could see this man would appeal to women, when he was duly shaved and cleaned up. Maybe even without that - maybe as he was now - who could tell?

Douet answered, 'Don't know what you bloody mean!'

Audran sighed inwardly. He had to let Douet go. Right now, anything else would be a waste of time. This was going to be a long slog, and a random chance.

Chapter Thirty-four

He came down the stairs, outlined against the light of the trap-door, and she tried to get to her feet, but the pain was too powerful: it gripped her and pulled her down on the beaten earth floor. She tried to call to him, but the sound came as a whimpering.

'God, it stinks here!'

There was a crashing metallic sound and she saw a chrome bucket gleaming in the ray of light. Beside it was a jug of water and a plate with some food scraps heaped on it.

'Toni - please - '

He hit her across the face.

'Shut up! I don't want to hear your whining again, you filthy cow!'

She didn't try to tell him, after that, how she wished that she were dead, that he would kill her.

That had, of course, also occurred to Toni. 'I should do it,' he said to himself when he got up out of the foul air of the cellar. 'I should do it!'

But the policeman in the Monkey had frightened him. Supposing the police found him - found her?

They never would! But all the same ... he tried to weigh things up. If he kept her alive for a bit, it would always be easy to frighten her into keeping her mouth shut, whereas her dead body - yes, dead, Marie would be mute testimony, beyond reach of his threats for ever.

In any case, there was something else he wanted. The thought of the woman down there, helpless, forced to accept whatever he subjected her to, gave him a sense of excitement whenever he thought about it. Something totally at his mercy.

Contemplating his face in the piece of mirror where he shaved, he saw that he had become red-eyed, almost wild-looking. 'Have to watch it,' he thought, 'I look different, somehow.'

He would have to be careful. But that thought didn't impede the feeling he had, the exultation that seemed to flow through him.

'Served her bloody right - to get rid of it! She tried to trap me - that was all. Well, she can pay the price now. That's all I'm doing - making her pay the price.' It made up for the humiliation he had suffered at the hands of that bastard in the Monkey. He would get his own back for that, anyway, but for the moment, he just let the thought of the woman who lay literally beneath his feet go coursing through his mind. He could do to her whatever he liked - anything.

He knew now that was what the old place had offered to him. The possibility to do exactly what he wanted. The cellar made him sick in a way, the smell was so disgusting now, shit and stale blood, rotting. Yet the dark secret place was what he wanted. A place where no one could find him, ever.

He didn't want to go to the Monkey again. When he went out, it was to a supermarket on the edge of town, where he bought a bottle of Scotch.

A police motorcyclist, huddled in waterproofs against the steady rain, caught the number-plate in the car-park and double-checked it. There'd been a special request. Information only, no need to apprehend. He noted the direction the bike took when it spun round and out onto the road and left a message on Audran's mobile.

Chapter Thirty-five

Marie, in the depths of her despair, scrabbled in the darkness, and touched the edge of the water-bucket. She dipped her hand in, her palm scooped ready. There was no water left. Time passed, with no markers except the reactions in her own body. At first, she had a burning thirst which constantly tormented her, but, pressing her hand against the cellar wall, she felt the old brickwork running with damp. It took her a long time before she could bring herself to do it, but eventually she did, twisting her neck round, stretching out her tongue, licking the rough bricks like a dog. It was foul, it scraped her tongue, but eventually it quenched her thirst. She no longer seemed to feel hunger - there had been pangs, not just sensations of wanting food, but cramps and spasms which had doubled her over. They had passed, and now she felt only nausea.

It was not completely dark: during the day, there was a thin rim of light around the ill-fitting door at the top of the steps and her eyes were becoming like those of a night-creature, readier to see in darkness than in light.

At first she had called out to him, over and over again. But she had heard no movement above her head for a long time now, no footsteps or creaks as he moved over the old floors.

He was gone, and there was no point in calling any longer. Was anyone looking for her?

She thought her father came down the stairs. 'Run away from home, would you? Who the hell cares?'

She shrank against the wall, feeling her weakness, her powerlessness.

'I am going to die here,' she thought, drifting again into the present.

The weakness was almost a relief, for it brought with it a kind of light-headedness. She imagined the world over her head, the drinkers in the Monkey, the tourists wandering up and down the long straight streets. She had no idea how long she had been here now - days and nights had fused together, except for the crack of light around the door at the top of the stairs. What if he never came back?

But there was something else, something that made her think he would, and almost made her fear that more than being left to die.

There was something in him that enjoyed seeing her there. So, when she heard footsteps at the top of the stairs, she tried instinctively to press her body into the cold wet wall. Her head was against the rough old brickwork and by some vibration through the earth she heard the distant reverberating sound of freedom, far away, yet travelling to her through the ground itself: the clip-clopping of a horse's hoofs. She screamed then, long and loud, in one last act of desperation, not knowing where she found the strength, her mouth cracking, her lips bleeding, and afterwards sank down again.

Beyond the trees, the riders trotted on, unhearing.

Chapter Thirty-six

Cecile got off the bus and walked steadily towards the end of Broad Street. She was beginning to get familiar with the main streets of Oxford: it was, after all, a very small city at the heart. Just a little medieval town.

At the end of the street she followed notices, and turned in between great columns at the top of a graceful flight of steps, where she pushed her way through heavy doors to find herself in a high room full of daylight from windows on two sides. The procedure was elaborate, but after various bits of paper, including her passport and a letter from Edward Cairns, the lawyer at Lincoln's Inn with whom she had once studied international law, had been produced, she found herself in possession of a ticket for the Bodleian Library. The reading room for modern manuscripts was on the other side of Broad Street, and there a very affable tall man with an open pleasant face helped her to fill in a request for the papers. 'They'll be here in an hour or so.'

She had coffee at a nearby pub in the meantime. The place had a notice board plastered with advertisements for concerts, plays and jazz festivals. As she explored the depths of the pub further, she found it concealed several small wood-panelled rooms, almost empty, including a back bar fitted with a bookcase which sported a row of battered hardback books and a torn brown and white paperback translation of the *Iliad*. There were a couple of serious-looking young men reading newspapers, the sheets held up defensively against any possible approach. Perfect! Only the British could manage this sort of thing - and when you found it, it was wonderful, absolutely anti-social, utter peace and quiet.

When she went back to the Bodleian, the notebooks were ready for her, neatly set out, and she settled down and began to read. She became so absorbed that she almost forgot her appointment, but just in time glanced up at the clock and realised it was nearly twelve o'clock. She obeyed the instructions posted on her desk, taking the bound notebooks back to the staff desk for safe-keeping when she left her seat, and pausing to ask the pleasant young man for directions to Chancellor's College. 'Just five minutes down the street on your left.'

So she was barely a minute or two late when she presented herself at an ivy-riddled lodge. The porter, eyeing her up as a tourist, no doubt, was at first unwilling to come to the glass box at the entrance, and when he eventually did so, leaned forward with an expression of immense strain, as if preparing to attempt to comprehend a barely human babble. He seemed surprised by Cecile's command of English, and dialled a number on an internal phone, listened to a voice quacking at the other end for a moment or two, and then turned to the visitor and said, with a complete change of manner, 'Yes, madam, if you go round the first quad, through that door on the right in the corner and up the staircase, Professor Sanderson's rooms are on the first floor.'

They were light and airy rooms, amounting to a large apartment, white-painted, with mullioned panes and deep window-seats overlooking another, tiny, courtyard. In the window embrasure stood an inlaid table bearing a pile of manuscript and a vase with sprays of small flowers, lilac and white, artless, almost as if picked from the wild. The light tangling greenery that embraced the windows seemed to fill the room with freshness, and there was barely a sound from the outside world. They might have been deep in the heart of the country, in some old private house. 'This is it,' thought Cecile, 'This is the real privilege. To live like this in the middle of a city, with servants to dish up the meals and clean the rooms. This is how no one has lived since the eighteenth century, except for the very rich, and even they can't buy it any longer.'

The woman sitting behind the long desk laden with books got up and came to meet her. 'Ah, madame, please have a seat. I understand you wanted to speak to me about one of my pupils, Marina Cassatt. But please, I want to make it clear right at the start, that anything to do with our students' private lives - their medical treatment, for example, or their academic progress, is confidential.'

'Yes, it is better to be direct, Professor. That way there is less room for misunderstanding. However, I did speak to Marina at Versailles.'

'She told me about the ... the incident there.'

Professor Sanderson had greyish hair flowing over her shoulders and a long, loose dress with some pattern of fruit and flowers in beige and rust colours; the full skirt settled round her as she sank down into her chair again, motioning Cecile to a seat between two precarious piles of books balanced on a velvet-covered sofa. She folded her plump white arms on the desk, and Cecile noted the remarkable eyes, at odds with the natural atmosphere and the flowing garment. They were small and round, almost like those of a stuffed toy, yet searching her visitor's face quite relentlessly. It was one of the few times in her life when Cecile felt she was undergoing a hostile scrutiny, almost as if she were under enemy observation. But after a moment or two, the eyes seemed to have taken in their fill, the mouth relaxed, and Professor Sanderson commented, 'I suppose, if you have taken the trouble to come all the way to Oxford, it must be an important matter.'

'Yes, and I'll be seeing Marina herself later. I phoned her, and we've arranged to meet. But there is something more. You see, the dismissal of Marina's story as untrue - that, I imagine, must have done quite a lot of damage to her.'

'It was very distressing all round. I will say, madame, that we are very worried about the possibility that Marina might abandon her academic career. Of course, it is our prime concern to keep her here, in Chancellor's. She is a very clever young woman. The college needs young people who have such academic potential.'

'Professor, I formed the opinion that Marina's account of the Versailles incident merited further investigation and I have given instructions for certain measures to be taken in France. I think there is a good possibility that we may find evidence to support her account of events.'

'That she really saw a murder at Versailles? Why, then, what about Blenheim?'

Professor Sanderson's mouth had opened in astonishment.

'You seem very surprised, Professor? But of course, because one incident is true, the other one need not be so. Proof of one will not necessarily verify the other.'

'You are a very rational person, Madame Galant. Of course, it would be a terrible thing if a murder had indeed occurred in France. But on the other hand -'

'On the other hand, it would certainly be a, what do you say? - a vindication of her state of mind, at least, at the time she was at Versailles.'

'Yes, a vindication, absolutely!' The Professor's tone was enthusiastic. 'And that would do her so much good. You see, she has begun to say that she is not worthy to go on with the work - and she really must not abandon that thesis! That's what I have been trying to tell her. But if she thinks she has been fantasising, if she doubts her mental state, her capacity for rational thought, then she may leave Oxford altogether, and give up her place at this college. You know, she came from a state school and an ordinary home - she is the first member of her family to go to university, so there was no privilege in her background. And she is a first-class student. I can't say any more - it would be unfair to her, a violation of privacy. But please believe me, I do hope that you will be able to prove that she wasn't mistaken. Her career may depend on it.'

'I understand you perfectly, Professor. I myself had a struggle to get my education and my professional qualifications, believe me.'

There was a pause. Cecile looked out of the window, seeing in her mind's eye something so different that it scarcely seemed to exist on the same planet, a windswept and dusty tower block, rubbish whirling in its draughty entrances, the blazing sun beating down mercilessly on its stained cement hinterlands, the human figures that scurried like ants around its base. I was one, she thought, and my mother still is, one of those nameless hurrying creatures living at the bottom of the heap, those who do not count, who struggle and beat against their surroundings and sometimes get out and leave the sink into which we were thrown. Do we spend all the rest of our lives struggling to keep from falling back, convincing ourselves that we belong somewhere else?

Professor Sanderson said, 'It's not uncommon, with women students, for them to feel that they really have no place here, that they're somehow imposters. It's an environment that was created by men, after all, by them and for them. That's what the college system is all about, creating all these little bonded groups. But we do try to look after them - the women, I mean. Get them through and launched into the world. She could be a high flier, Marina, if she sticks to it and finishes her thesis. She'd be a candidate for my job, eventually! But there's something else that we can't avoid. If she was telling the truth about Versailles ...'

'Then what happened at Blenheim? If I can find out that also - that's what I want to do, here, Professor. Find out what happened. That's my job, you see, an enquiry into the truth. But I came to see you because I just wanted to have, from an expert opinion, an idea of her academic standing. Thank you, you've clarified that for me, and the College's attitude to high-fliers.'

'Oh, naturally, we want to protect them.'

Cecile got up. Professor Sanderson stood up and came round the desk to open the heavy door with a hefty tug: there was another beyond it, even heavier-looking, but that was chained open.

'There's one more thing,' said the Professor, putting her plump little face round the wooden door. 'Perhaps I shouldn't be saying this - but her boyfriend, Luke, I believe, his name is - '

There was a certain amount of disdain in her tone.

'Oh, yes,' said Cecile. 'I met in him in France, he seemed sensible enough.'

'I feel, that is, the College feels, well, that he is not exactly encouraging Marina's academic career. I don't want to say any more - in fact I shouldn't be telling you this, but I thought I'd just mention it. And he didn't seem terribly upset after her accident - she apparently ran into the road and was hit by a van or a car, but there were no witnesses and she didn't remember much about it. We don't think Luke Elmer is the best of influences, put it like that.'

The door banged shut behind her with an authentic-sounding medieval thud.

The college was like a miniature fortress, full of cells and towers that could be sealed off from the world, thought Cecile, as she made her way down the stairs, across the quad and back into the world of roaring traffic outside the gates.

Chapter Thirty-seven

Pierre Maubourg and his wife sat on their small balcony, from which they could see a patch of the glorious glimmering azure of the Riviera, a blue so pure, so luminous, that sometimes it was possible, even now, to forget the roads, the tourism, and all the other disfigurements, human and architectural, that the twentieth century had left in its wake.

He looked across at Violetta. Her beautiful face was looking calmly out to the little speck of sea, the fine lines of her high cheekbones relaxed, her dark cloud of soft hair blowing gently round her face in the breeze. This was one of the times when she was reconciled to being the wife of an inspector who wasn't going to ascend much further through the ranks or take the criminal world by storm.

Her husband was an old lag of a policeman, so as to speak. He rarely talked to her nowadays about his work: when they were first married, she had been excited by every case he had dealt with, and he in his turn had made dramatic accounts for her - not fictionalising, never that, but telling her about the characters involved, the risks he took. Now, the risks were as commonplace as the headlines that screamed 'Agent murdered during investigation!' Or 'Officer accused of corruption, court told.'

There were many things they no longer talked about. His desperate suspicions that she might have a lover, the frantic accusations, the calm and laughing denials, those were behind them these days. They made love sometimes, went to concerts now and then, on the rare occasion when he could get off duty. Sometimes they even behaved like Cannois, and strolled together along the flower-lined boulevard of the Croisette, or, during the Film Festival, went together to some star-studded film-show for which he had been given complimentary tickets. She had enjoyed seeing Julia Roberts and Tom Cruise at a première: it was the kind of thing that made Cannes seem worthwhile again, the place she had loved when they had first moved here.

'How can I blame her?' he thought. And then, 'For what? Does she still see him?'

He had never known the name of her lover.

Their daughter, Rachelle, now preparing for university, came out on to the balcony with glasses of chilled lemonade.

'Thank you, darling.' Violetta took the tray from Rachelle's sturdy brown hands. 'I hope you won't be working all evening. Come out here and join us for a while.' There was an edge of irritation to her voice.

Maubourg and his daughter avoided catching one another's eyes - they both knew this would increase that sharpness. 'Oh, *Maman*, I can't, I said I'd go round to Martine's - we're helping each other revise, you know.'

'Very well. But you so rarely have the chance to spend an evening with your father. He's always on duty.'

Rachelle's expression showed a glimmer of pain at the way in which Violetta had manipulated the conversation, but then her young face softened forgivingly as she looked at her mother.

Why do we love her, thought Maubourg, in spite of her bitching? Because she is so beautiful, so graceful to look at in everything she does? Simply that? Can physical beauty really alter the way we feel about someone? Is it so strong, so powerful? Rachelle had not inherited her intellect from her mother, that was certain.

But then he thought to himself that, although Violetta wasn't clever, she had a certain acuteness, a ruthlessness, even, that made up for any deficit in intellect. Often, when they had been younger, she had cut through his elaborate accounts of his professional life, as if with a clean-bladed knife. 'But, obviously, he's the one to go after!' Or, 'Watch that one - he'll put a dagger in your back!'

An incident from the past came into his head as he looked down from their balcony into the little palm-lined garden next door, where the neighbour's old white cat was curling itself into a ball.

When Rachelle was a child, she had had a smoky-grey Persian kitten called Mimi, two great owl-like gold eyes in a ball of fluff. It loved dark corners and crept into all kinds of tiny hot spaces to sleep. Into the airing-cupboard, between the hot-water pipes - Mimi was constantly being rescued, usually at Rachelle's instigation, sometimes against its will.

One day he had got into the car - it was the old one - and as he tuned the ignition there was a dull thudding noise and a terrible little cry, like a scream, so close to him that he jumped. He knew instantly, without having to think about it, what had happened, because he had heard of it happening before and filed it away as a minor horror, perhaps an urban myth, that he hoped he would never encounter.

Now he had encountered it, he found he couldn't deal with it. He got out of the car and went up into the flat, running up the stairs because the lift was between floors.

He and Violetta spoke like conspirators, because Rachelle was still in her bedroom and might overhear, a whispered conversation that ended with his wife grabbing a towel from the bathroom and running down to the car.

There his wife did what he hadn't the courage to do: opened the bonnet, and lifted out the small bundle of fur and blood, looked at it, wrapped it in the towel and put it on the back seat. Then she got into the car, and, biting her lips, tentatively started the engine, and when it fired she tore out of the car-park and drove the kitten to the vet, who pronounced that it was still alive, just, but the fan-belt had slashed into the fragile little skull. An injection gave it a merciful despatch.

And it was Violetta who broke the news to Rachelle - a censored version of an accident, that didn't include Mimi climbing up underneath the car and choosing the warm engine-casing as a suitable place for a snooze.

For all her apparent fragility, Violetta could deal with situations, he thought. She could sometimes make swift decisions. And she had usually been right

He thought, now, he could talk to her again.

She had known him long enough. She said, 'There's something worrying at you, Pierre. Something more than usual, I mean.'

He told her, after he had heard the sound of the lift taking Rachelle down to the bottom of the block of flats.

Strange, how Violetta, who had always disliked that particular source of his anxiety which was troubling him now, perhaps even felt some kind of rivalry, should be the means of resolving the situation.

'Well, he may be able to manipulate everything from inside a prison cell. But he's trapped inside prison, too, isn't he? She can get away - she has, and he can't.'

He looked at her, the implications of what she had said dawning in his mind. Her huge eyes, set in their arched hollows like long jewels, gazed back without blinking. 'After all, he's still a public menace, even in jail. You'd just be stopping the rot at the source.'

Sometimes, she cut straight through all the difficulties and made things so easy.

Chapter Thirty-eight

As Cecile inserted her key in the front door of Mrs. Robertson's premises, the lady herself popped out, in some state of excitement. 'We'll be on TV tonight!' she called, and then amplified it. 'On television! There's a programme about Blenheim Palace!'

So there was, and a little later Cecile lay back on her bed and experimented with the controls of the television set placed on a high shelf before her. Sure enough, there came a programme which she followed perfectly well, about the Duke of Marlborough and his employees and the harmonious relationships which prevailed. To her astonishment, a woman appeared and told the camera how privileged she felt to have permission to go horse-riding in that enormous expanse of grounds. Privileged? Who the hell was privileged here?

Cecile thought of the hunt she had seen. She had wondered how they hung on to the bloody nature of the reality beneath the velvet lawns, that same brutal ugly truth of power which disfigured Versailles: now she saw one of its disguises.

She got out her mobile phone and pressed the buttons.

'Have there been any results of the investigation at your end?' she prompted the voice at the other end.

'No, madame ... nothing here.'

'What about the stretches of water in the grounds?'

'It has not been possible to ... to make arrangements, as yet.'

'I instructed dragging!'

'Yes, madame, unfortunately there were ... environmental problems.'

'What environmental problems.'

'Er, I understand, concerning the disturbing of fish stocks.'

'Well,' said Cecile nastily, remembering Marina Cassatt's rescued carp, left to die in a slowly draining basin, 'If there is any serious objection from leading piscologists their reports will be taken into account and a case claiming reparation may be prepared by the authorities at the Château. After the lake has been dragged.'

She did not wait to hear any more.

Walking in the town to get some fresh air, she noted an inn menu again. Rosette of Melon with Mango Salsa, Warm Fingers of Marinated Salmon. There was a notice nearby: "For 700 years we have offered shelter to the wayfarer, rich and poor."

Not to me, she thought, and had an omelette in a café.

In any case, it was time to occupy her mind with something more serious, she told herself as she appreciated the salad that accompanied it. When she got home, she took out her notebooks and made some plans for the next day. But she went to bed early, after the evening phone calls to Daniel and Florence, pulling out the aerial in front of Mrs. Robertson's window, as though to better traverse the ether between here and France, which suddenly seemed so distant.

'Darling, how are you getting on there?'

Daniel was staying on the campus at the University of Saint-Quentin near Versailles, where he was lecturing in computation.

'It's fine,' came his voice, loving, loved, familiar, out of the little perforated black slab of plastic. 'How are you getting on?'

'There's something I want you to look up for me, if you could. Probably worth looking through some old Paris directories.'

'Is it to do with the Versailles business?'

'Yes, but the answer to this may be in Paris.'

After she'd spelled out the name, they talked for a few more minutes, things of trivia, of reassurance, longing. When they ended the conversation, she felt better able to make the call to Florence, the small voice excited, answering straight away, so perhaps she had been waiting by the phone. 'I'm bringing you home a story about a little girl and a white rabbit. It's a very famous one - an English story.'

'Tell me now, Maman!'

'Well, maybe I'll just start it. I think the rabbit is wearing a check jacket.' Opening the copy of 'Alice', she began to read the famous first sentence.

'Alice was beginning to get very tired of sitting by her sister on the bank ...'

After a few minutes, Florence broke in, 'Mummy, is it a magical story?'

'Yes, it is.'

'Is it only English people see magical things? Like Harry Potter?'

The voice sounded drowsy.

'I don't think so, darling. I'm sure we all do - think of the *Contes de Fées*.'

Louis's voice breaking in.

'Cecile? She's getting sleepy. Time to go to bed, sweetheart.'

'No, I want Mummy's story...'

'Tomorrow, darling. I'll ring you again.'

Were they becoming an empty ritual, these calls? 'As advertised on television.' A mere perfunctory electronic version of a meaningless goodnight kiss? What use was a mother who wasn't there in the night for her child?

'Expect some repercussions from the shock,' the doctor had said, after pronouncing her physically fit when she left the hospital. 'Night fears, bad dreams, maybe. Flooding - re-living the moment of the explosion. They will go, eventually. Get plenty of rest.'

She lay awake, seeing the small face floating before her in the darkness, and finally put the television on again, very quietly, so as not to disturb any other guests, and watched some late night movie in fifties technicolor till she fell asleep.

Chapter Thirty-nine

The heavy barred gate clanged shut behind Maubourg, who stood in the concrete yard waiting to be conducted through the next level of security. The warder beside him inserted a swipe-card and then pressed a sequence of keys on a pad next to the door, and Maubourg passed through into a different world. White and steel, antiseptic, the soft whirring of filters, no windows, no natural light anywhere, no sound from the outside world. Perpetual imprisonment: a hell of emptiness.

They passed a series of blank steel doors. 'How do you monitor them?' asked the policeman.

'Cameras in the ceilings.' He slid a wall-panel aside and a screen showed them the scene within the cell before which they had paused. It looked almost monastic, thought Maubourg, almost innocent. A man was seated at a desk in a barely-furnished room, deeply absorbed in a book. Almost a normal world, yet the prisoner suddenly turned and raised his eyes upwards and Maubourg saw his face in close-up on the screen and, in spite of all his experience and training, started with horror at the simple elemental hatred in the face. The features, swollen with drugs, seemed fixed in an animal mask, the lips drawn back in a permanent snarl, the eyes glaring with a deep wolfine gleam.

Neither man in the corridor commented. The warder was laconic, trained, probably, to say as little as possible, even to those who had cleared all security levels. They both knew that this was the territory of the beyond-human. There was a creature held here who had killed a woman in the depths of winter, hidden her body on a deserted mountainside and returned night after night to cut out and eat parts of the semi-frozen soft tissues, crouching over the body beneath the cold starry sky. There were things here beyond the invention of the darkest of writers.

But they had reached the end of the corridor, and the warder leaned forward and spoke into a microphone set in the door.

'Stand up!'

The screen outside the cell revealed a tall man, thin and stooping, with greasy grey hair, who got off the bed and slowly obeyed the instruction.

'Call me when you've finished.' He indicated the buzzer in Maubourg's jacket pocket. 'There's another of those in the door, and I'll be close anyway, but there's not much likelihood of attack from this one. No record of it, anyway, though of course that never means it won't come. He's allowed association with other prisoners, anyway. Like most of the drug-dealers. '

But as Maubourg passed into the cell, the occupant was quiet. Their conversation was brief.

A few minutes passed before the inspector pressed his buzzer. 'Results first,' he said, as he turned to leave.

The silence was eerie, so well insulated was the little room that even the footsteps of the warder making no sound as they approached the door.

'What it must it be like to know that you would never emerge from this living death?' he asked himself, as they retraced their steps through the prison.

It wasn't a question that Montvallon wasted any time on, when they talked about it later. Montvallon shifted his heavy bulk on the front seat of the Peugeot and lit another Gauloise. 'Look, chief,' he said to Maubourg, 'I wouldn't give him any choice.' There was a brief pause, then he corrected himself. 'I wouldn't give either of the bastards any choice.'

Chapter Forty

Élise lay on her bed, staring at the light, which was shrouded in a tiny shade. She had done what she could - if anything had happened to Marie, it was her own fault for going with such a bastard. She should have known what he was like. 'I knew, after all,' said Élise to herself. 'I could tell.'

She looked out of the window: the rain was heavier now, streaking the pane.

It was ridiculous, that business about going to live out in the countryside. If she had ever seen someone who belonged on the pavements of Paris, it was Marie. And as for Toni - 'he belongs there like a rat belongs in the sewers,' thought Élise.

But all the same, she lay there, staring at the ceiling because it was too wet to go even as far as the kiosk and get a packet of cigarettes. She rummaged through her bag, but had no luck.

She tried to put Marie out of her mind. But it came back to her, that plaintive sound of her friend's voice. 'If I went missing - would you look for me?'

'I did my best, Marie,' said Élise, and heard the sound of her own voice. Damn, had she started talking out loud?

Where the hell could she look, anyway? Marie had never said where it was - in fact, she had probably never known, exactly. There was a lot of woodland round here, open spaces, parks, a huge area. Élise supposed it had all once belonged to them, in the Château, the King and Queen, riding round in carriages while the rest of them starved. God damn their souls.

There was a knock at the door. Élise wasn't expecting any callers. She jumped up and looked out of the window, seeing the top of a man's blond head. Didn't look like a copper.

He pulled his collar up against the rain and called out, against the rain driving into his face, 'Mademoiselle Barrau?' She called down, 'All right, I'm coming.'

She didn't really think he had come to see her - well, not in that way - just didn't want to keep him out in the rain. He had a nice face, open, with the hair in a quiff like Tin-Tin.

The name, Daniel something, didn't mean anything to her, but he evidently knew who she was, and she was starting to push the door shut when he said, 'No, I'm not from the police. The judge, Madame Galant, asked me to have word with you.'

Élise's arm dropped away from the latch. She was still wary, but said, 'Better come in, I suppose. But I haven't got anything to say. I've told her everything I could remember. You got any fags?'

'I'll get you some from the kiosk. What brand?'

He was back in a few minutes with the Marlboro.

Inside her room, they went over what Marie had told her, yet again.

'But all she said was they had this place with trees around - just somewhere, just some place he liked. I don't think she even knew herself where it was.'

'And she didn't say anything that gave you any idea? How long it took to get there, for instance?'

'No. Only that it was old. She liked that.'

'Please, just think about it. Everything she said - anything that might give you a clue.'

But there was nothing.

After he had gone, she thought about it. Maybe there had been something, but she couldn't think what.

She got into bed and went to sleep.

At about three o'clock in the morning there was a tremendous storm and Élise realised the window, the one through which she had called down to Daniel, was still open. The rain was coming in, lashing at an angle.

She got up and closed it, went back to bed and sat there, hugging her knees.

Well, it could wait till morning.

Chapter Forty-one

The pleasure of settling down at the desk recalled for Cecile her student days; the atmosphere, quiet, studious, heads all bowed over their separate worlds.

She opened one of the four notebooks in front of her, and to her surprise found it was a typewritten record. Copies of correspondence and statements dating over a period of years, from 1901 to 1924, made by Miss Moberly of St. Hugh's College, and safely lodged in the Bodleian Library.

1901 - that was when Miss Moberly and Miss Jourdain, the two English ladies from Oxford claimed to have seen ghosts in the grounds of the Château of Versailles. And 1924 - what did that signify? She would leave that for the moment.

The ladies, it seemed, had their supernatural experiences in August, but it was not for a week that they had discussed them. And not till Nov.12th of that year that they mentioned them to any outsider. But then they had embarked on telling everyone in their circle of acquaintances, it seemed, and very distinguished acquaintances they were. The first two volumes of the notebooks contained copies of letters from Lord and Lady this, the Honourable so-and-so, the Bishop of Southwark, the Countess Waldegrave ... all confirming that the two ladies had spoken of the events at Versailles to them, and their own explanation was that they had somehow entered within the mind of Marie-Antoinette when she was still alive.

All that meant, of course, was that there was ample evidence that the two had told people that they had experienced a supernatural adventure, not that they had actually seen any ghosts. The experience itself had been recorded in their book, 'An Adventure', published in 1911.

In 1911? Why so long a gap?

The reason seemed quite plausible. They had spoken of it to many people who said they should put their testimony on permanent record for a wider audience. Eventually, they had done so. Fine. Yet there was something else that seemed strange - why had there been such a long gap, between August and November of 1901, before Moberly and Jourdain had apparently spoken of the matter even to each other? It just did not seem at all probable that two people should undergo such an experience as revisiting a scene from the past and fail to mention it for three whole months. The obvious answer to that was that at the time they had thought their experiences perfectly normal and it was three months before the suggestion entered their heads that they might have been at all supernatural.

Odder still, as Cecile perused the pages of the several editions of 'An Adventure', was the failure to actually cite references or evidence. It was all presented as though they had been academically very scrupulous, yet there were such obvious gaps. Jourdain, for example, did not reveal in which library she had seen that old map which appeared to back up their story. They had great connections, these women, heads of Oxford Colleges, bishops, nobility - so they presumably had thought they didn't need to bring proof: their word would be believed. The reason that the story had acquired so much fame and success was due to the unimpeachable character of the two women, and the research carried out by Eleanor Jourdain to prove that they had seen things not actually visible in 1901, but which would have been there during the time of Marie-Antoinette.

The thing was to forget the titles, forget all about the bishops and the baronets, and concentrate on what had actually happened.

On that hot August day the two Oxford ladies had walked a long way through the grounds of Versailles, and rambled down the long walk and then to the right, towards the Petit Trianon, which they had approached from the back of the building, a balanced and harmonious classical structure, the façades of which were all very similar. There was a formal garden on the west side and a courtyard to the south, through which was the main entrance. It was conceived of as a 'country retreat', where the King and Queen could play at the simple life. Except that by most people's standards it was a miniature palace.

Approaching this building, the two ladies claimed to have seen a miniature bridge over a cascade, and to have gone through woods which were no longer extant, and to have seen an ornamental kiosk, all of which had existed only in the past and did not appear on modern maps. They had noticed gardeners dressed in old-fashioned uniforms, and passed by rough-looking ground which was now smooth turf. A sinister-looking fellow had spoken to them, and Miss Jourdain had seen a lady sketching in the grounds, a woman wearing long full skirts and a delicate scarf around her neck, whom she identified with Marie-Antoinette herself. And then they had encountered another man, who appeared to have emerged from a doorway that no longer existed.

She read through all the documents carefully, and then stretched her legs beneath the desk. Time to go back to Chancellor's College.

Chapter Forty-two

'Let's just run over what they claimed to have seen,' said Cecile. 'Just as they told it in their book.' She had her notebook in front of her, and was squinting slightly in the sunshine. 'I've been too long indoors,' she thought to herself. She added aloud, 'I'm so glad you were willing to see me - you know, I've found this a fascinating puzzle. And I promise to keep our talk just to this old story, to past history.'

Opposite her Marina, curled up in a bamboo chair, sipped tea slowly. She was looking much better than she had done in Versailles, Cecile thought, as if she had come to terms with something. Shaky, but wanting to concentrate on something outside her own emotions. Her eyes still looked red-rimmed, but they were dry, and her hair had been carefully combed. Around them, in the garden of her college, shady trees stretched overhead, and a climbing rose straggled up an old wall.

'I think we need to start with their state of mind,' she said in response to Cecile. 'One of the things they admit is that there was almost a trance-like quality about the experience, and Moberly at any rate experienced a very severe feeling of depression.'

She leafed through the book in her lap and quoted, "There was a feeling of depression and loneliness about the place." And again, they turned from a lane to the direction of the Trianon, and Moberly says, "an extraordinary depression had come over me, which, in spite of every effort to shake it off, steadily deepened."

'Yes, she does give the impression that something was affecting her mental state,' said Cecile, thoughtfully. 'Almost a hypnotic quality, I should say. "Everything suddenly looked unnatural, therefore unpleasant; even the trees behind the building seemed to have become flat and lifeless, like a wood worked in tapestry. There were no effects of life and shade, and no wind stirred the trees. It was all intensely still."

'What did she see then? - oh, yes, the two men.' Marina took up the thread. 'A man she found very repulsive, with a rough, dark complexion - and another, who came was handsome, yet red-faced as if through intense exertion, very excited.'

They caught each other's eyes, and both women laughed.

'I don't suppose for a minute she'd ever experienced it! She was obviously a very virtuous woman,' said Marina.

'Primal scene? The father in the sexual act, observed by the child?'

'That might be a Freudian diagnosis, certainly!'

'Yes, my husband mentioned that. Anyway, she says this fellow urged them to take a certain direction towards a little bridge over a miniature cascade which fell down a little ravine. Then they got to the house, and there they saw - none other than Queen Marie-Antoinette herself!

'To be fair,' commented Marina, 'they said at first it was merely a lady, seated on a stool and sketching. Moberly described it as not an attractive face.'

'So maybe she wasn't romanticising too much,' responded Cecile.

'Or maybe she was a clever story-teller - knew exactly where to draw the line. After all, there are portraits of Marie-Antoinette, and she wasn't particularly beautiful.'

'In fact,' said Cecile thoughtfully, assembling the information in her mind, as she would for the dossier her clerk would compile if this were a current case, 'when Moberly saw a picture of the Queen, she claimed that only then did she recognise the woman she had seen sketching. That can't have been the first portrait of the Queen she had seen, surely. They had gone round the house, through the Hall of Mirrors and the State Apartments.' Cecile raked her memory. 'There must have been some pictures of the Queen there. You can see them today, at any rate.'

Marina had evidently done her research. 'And they were hanging there in 1901. I've looked up old guidebooks and a catalogue of the art collection. At the time the two ladies went round, the picture gallery was full of portraits. Pictures of Marie-Antoinette, of the King, of the royal mistresses. They must have seen the Queen's apartments, her bedchamber with a white marble bust of her on the mantelpiece. Life-size paintings of her and her children. And Eleanor Jourdain wrote a book on the French Revolution. She must have done a lot of research about it. Miss Moberly must have known something about the period, too: her brother had written a prize poem about Marie-Antoinette. He must have had some history books for that! And there's a famous portrait of the Queen by Madame Vigée-Lebrun, which is reproduced in all the books about her - in engravings in the older ones.'

'So do you think that Moberly already had an idea of what the Queen looked like?'

'I think she must have formed an image of her, as they were going round,' said Marina, thoughtfully. 'But at the time, Moberly says she just thought that the dress of the lady she saw in the grounds was old-fashioned and unusual. Fichu collars were quite fashionable in the summer of 1901, and of course they were all wearing long skirts. Add a muslin collar and straw sun-hat, perhaps, to a wide-skirted dress and it would be quite like eighteenth-century costume, from a distance, anyway. Imagination would easily do the rest.'

'Anyway,' said Cecile, 'we get to the last peculiar event: they arrived at the Petit Trianon itself, and saw a man emerging from another building at right angles to it. A young man stepped out of a door and offered to show the ladies the way into the house. After that, they found a wedding-party going round the rooms, and things became perfectly normal again.'

'And a week later, Moberly asked Jourdain, "Do you think the Petit Trianon is haunted?" Jourdain amswered immediately, "Yes, I do."'

'Folie à deux,' murmured Cecile.'I recall something about that from the psychology course we had to do as students. That could be the explanation. It's when two people - or sometimes a whole family - share a powerful delusion. Often it's one dominating personality which takes over another, weaker, mind.'

'Do you think that's what happened here?'

'It might have been how it started. I think Moberly was a very intense, powerful personality, apart from being the older of the two, and the senior academic. But they both kept adding bits of embroidery. And some were quite absurd: three years later, Jourdain went to a performance of the Barber of Seville and declared some of the cast were dressed like the gardeners at Versailles, but with scarlet stockings!'

Marina leaned back and shielded her eyes against a ray of sun. 'Yes, I get the impression they were both highly imaginative. And Jourdain made a second visit to Versailles - she was the one who ran round doing all the research, while Moberly stayed in Oxford. Eleanor Jourdain went to France alone, the following January. That time she went straight to the Petit Trianon. And again, things got very strange. "As if I had crossed a circle and was suddenly in a line of influence." That time she found herself in a wood so thick she couldn't see through the trees and saw a cloaked man slipping about, and heard rustling, as if a group of people in silk dresses was nearby, and music playing softly.'

'She has a turn for drama, our Miss Jourdain,' exclaimed Cecile.

'Yes - she connects it with an incident in the history of Versailles, when a servant came running to the Trianon with a letter warning Marie-Antoinette that the Paris mob would be at the gates of Versailles in an hour's time.'

'Just a legend?'

Marina answered her carefully. 'There's no evidence for it, certainly, not that I've been able to find in my research. Jourdain went to the Trianon on many occasions after that, but she claims the grounds were quite different. They both said the Belvedere and the Temple of Love, the only structures that correspond to the kiosk they saw, were actually quite different. And that the only bridge was also quite unlike the one they had seen.'

'But the Belvedere, the Temple of Love and their kiosk - they were all similar buildings.'

'Yes, little ornamental temples with pillars and balustrades. Their 'kiosk' sounds like a combination of the other two - maybe they remembered them in a confused way and mixed up their features.'

'That would have been easy enough to do. They went back together, didn't they?' asked Cecile.

'In the summer of 1904. It all seemed changed - the kiosk had gone, as had the bridge over the ravine. Where the lady had been sitting, there was a well-grown rhododendron bush. And the thick woods had vanished.'

Turning towards Marina, Cecile looked at the serious young face, gazing down at an illustrated guide to Versailles that lay open on her lap. But the girl suddenly looked at the older woman. Cecile hadn't sufficiently disguised her own expression, the query that hung in her mind about recent events.

Marina flushed and got up, standing upright and tense.

'No - I'm not mad, you know! I don't fantasize! Of course they exist, the people I saw there!'

She stopped suddenly, pressing her hand over her mouth. Cecile looked at her pale, agitated face with some concern.

'I'm sorry - please sit down again! Perhaps I'm tiring you?'

'Yes - I want to rest now. I'm sorry I couldn't meet you in Woodstock- Luke didn't want me to see you at all, and maybe he was right after all. I thought it would be all right if we just talked about past history.'

'Tell me one more thing. Please. Just a few more minutes.'

Cecile's voice was quiet, yet there was something in it that was very compelling. Marina sat down slowly and looked round at the soft smooth green of the lawn, the rough old stone walls. She seemed to breathe more easily.

'Luke thought you were imagining things, didn't he? You see, what I don't understand is why he would do it. Luke, your boyfriend. Why he would let them hurt you like that? Let everyone think you were having delusions? Why should he feel like that?'

Marina stared at Cecile, and there was a shiny film of tears in her eyes as she said, 'I knew the truth long ago, deep inside, but I didn't ever want to admit it. Look at all this around here.'

She waved her hand towards their surroundings, the Gothic doorways, the tall pinnacled tower of the college chapel, the ranks of flower-beds in the distance where a gardener was hoeing between tumbling rose-bushes.

'Privilege, isn't it? You can't deny the privilege, to study in these surroundings - and you haven't seen the college library, or the dining-hall with the tables covered with silver for a guest night. It carries a tremendous impact, even now, to be at Oxford. This is still a terribly snobbish country, you know.'

'And he resented that?'

Marina seemed to sigh with relief. She fished out a hanky and blew her nose.

'I couldn't say any of this to the men. I don't think they would have understood, really. Because there are things none of them want to admit, even that Inspector Halley, and I felt he was on my side really. But yes, Luke always resented it.'

'He works in local government, I understand.'

'Yes, Luke has a good job. He works in the housing department. But he's not ...'

'Not intellectually a high-flier like you?'

'I wouldn't admit it for ages. I kept saying to myself that I wasn't really any brighter than him, it was just that I'd been fortunate, that I'd got accepted for Oxford, and then I had lucky questions in my finals so I got a first. I never had friends from College round, in case Luke felt awkward, and whenever his friends came, we never talked about - well about anything academic.'

'You must have felt very isolated?' Cecile felt a genuine concern for this confused young creature.

'I just felt that was the way it was - I'd got here by a fluke. But then, as I was finishing my thesis, well, they want you to start applying for fellowships, and Professor Sanderson said I stood a good chance, that I should have - '

'An excellent academic career ahead of you. Yes, I know, I've spoken to her.'

'So that meant I wouldn't be here just for a few years as a student. It would be a career, I would get a job on the academic ladder. Have you seen the rooms that the dons have here?'

Cecile recalled Professor Sanderson's long study, the Georgian windows, the panelling, the mahogany table laden down with books. It wasn't particularly well furnished, rather shabby, if she remembered rightly. But it was impressive, no doubt about that.

'It's a suite of rooms, she has, isn't it?' she asked Marina.

'Oh, yes, it's like an apartment on its own within the college.'

'Equality has only come so far.'

There was a pause and the two women regarded each other with some understanding.

'In more ways than one!' said Marina.'Anyway, I don't think Luke would be able to take it. The sort of world I would be in. Oh, I don't think Oxford and Cambridge are really any better than a lot of other universities, not as far as the teaching and the students are concerned. But these buildings, just the atmosphere - it makes people believe there's something very special here. And Luke wouldn't have been part of it.'

Cecile left the garden, walking slowly through the streets to Gloucester Green, where she could get a bus to Woodstock. It was market day, and there were other passengers loaded down with shopping, bulging bags of sprouts and apples, as well as the usual scattering of tourists.

She was thinking about Marina, because she sensed that there was still more, something that was kept hidden.

'It's like peeling away the layers of an onion, getting at the truth,' she thought, eying a straw basket full of greens.

A few minutes after Cecile had left, Marina Cassatt walked into Professor Sanderson's room.

'I can't keep quiet any longer,' she said. 'I think Madame Galant suspects there's more to it. I know in a way it's just to prove I was right, but I can't keep it secret any longer. I'm sorry!'

Tears were running down her face, and she found a crumpled tissue in a pocket.

'It's all right,' said Susan Sanderson. 'We were asking too much of you, I realise that. Especially now, after what you saw in Woodstock yesterday.'

'What shall we do?' Marina was still sobbing, though she was trying to stifle it.

Susan Sanderson lifted the phone on her desk and dialled for an outside line.

'We'll have to tell the police and take the consequences.'

Chapter Forty-three

Association was allowed, but under the strictest of supervision, and only for 'trusted' categories, so the small group moving slowly in the yard at Lyons was, in its way, very select. The fat man tried to shield his face from the sun whenever it struck down through the intermittent clouds, as though it would do him some injury, and he waddled with discomfort, as though his thighs were chafing together. He was, even on a prison diet, grossly corpulent and sweating at the most moderate exertion. The prison doctor had recommended exercise as a health move.

The guard on duty took a certain satisfaction as he peered at the close-circuit screen. He identified the fat man with the boss class: with those who made others come to them, and never put themselves on the line, to sweat or struggle. 'White Boy,' he said to his companion. 'Big man in gangland. Ran a lot of the nasty stuff along the Riviera. Got put away by a female, though.'

'In the police?'

'No, a *juge d'instruction* in Cannes. She never gives up on an investigation, they say. But they had to move her somewhere else afterwards. That fat bastard is after her, they say. Still has contacts.'

'Revenge? That's traditional, in these parts. That's what he wants, then?'

'Doubly. First because he was put inside, and second, because it was by a woman.'

Another prisoner came close to White Boy, who looked to be staggering with the unaccustomed movement. The second man put an arm round his shoulder.

'Ah, it's just the bastard's so gross. Can hardly walk - serve him bloody right. Look how the other sods suck up to him - even in here!'

The guards left White Boy to stagger round for a few minutes more, and then to stumble through the door of the recreation room. It was thus a good few minutes after the occurrence that anyone suspected there was something wrong, even after White Boy had fallen down ridiculously against the door, and later still when they found the wound. Or, more properly, they found the instrument still in the puncture wound, a type of long bodkin, of murderously thin and sharpened steel, with a neat hilt like a ladies' old-fashioned hat-pin, that was driven in up to the flesh and prevented the blood from pouring out. A slim thing, but it was long enough to have gone right into a chamber of the heart.

'Who the hell...?'

'Who was that bloke who got close to him? The one who put an arm round his shoulder, for Christ's sake?'

They re-ran the CCTV film, identified the helper. By that time, the cell was empty.

They did rush White Boy to surgery but his heart couldn't take the strain. He died under the anaesthetic.

'Bloody hell, near miss,' said Montvallon. 'They might have saved him.'

They were driving at night along the road to Monaco. A flight had been booked to Ecuador. In the back of the car, a man with grey, greasy hair, turned over his new passport.

'Boss? Mind telling me why?'

'I owed her. She covered my back when they were trying to get me. I stepped out of line to get that bastard henchman of White Boy's.'

'The one whose neck you broke?'

'Yeah.' And I owe madame le juge for something else, he thought. For not listening to the dirty gossip they were spreading about Violetta.

'Shit, you called in a lot of favours, boss.'

Yes, thought Maubourg, and I owe a lot of favours now, as well.

Chapter Forty-four

Élise had spent the night alone, though she could have gone back with one of the blokes from the Monkey, a barman who had always fancied her. She knew it, she and Marie had laughed about him. But now she felt frightened, as if there were something terrifying that had brushed very close to her, yet she didn't know what it was, couldn't identify its appearance. Anyone's company would have been better than lying alone, wondering if there were noises at the door, trying to think of where this feeling was coming from.

It was to do with Marie, she became certain, as she got up, sat in an armchair and pulled the duvet round her shoulders. She went over things again, everything that Marie had said to her. God, she'd been crazy about that bastard Toni, stupid woman! All the same, she was her friend. Marie hadn't had many friends - she'd had a pretty hard life, on the whole. Maybe that was why she seemed to have no judgement about men: she desperately wanted some affection, something to love.

Dawn came late on a greasy wet morning, but Élise was relieved to see the first light, as she lit another cigarette, and sat, smoking and thinking, trying to remember. Marie had wanted to know something - would Élise try to find her, if anything happened?

She dressed, put on a raincoat and went out for some coffee and a croissant, standing up at the counter.

There were no other customers at this hour of the morning, except for a few workmen who called in and went off with hot rolls and coffee. One or two of them looked at Élise curiously, and she stared at her finger-nails till they turned away.

The woman in the café was friendly enough. She was stretching over the counter, setting out her pastries with long tongs, but willing to talk.

'You look a bit rough. Are you feeling all right? There's a lot of flu about.'

'Yeah, I'm OK, thanks.'

There was a pause. The woman put a tray of almond tarts behind the glass screen.

Élise stood quietly for a few more minutes. The smells of cinnamon, of apples and pastry, the quiet orderly movements, were comforting.

'Tell me, would you try to find someone? I mean a friend, who's gone missing.'

The response was surprised, but interested, willing to consider the issue. It seemed the right thing to think about on a morning such as this.

'A man or a woman?'

Yes, that was a crucial question. Men, in Élise's experience, often wanted to go missing.

'Woman. I used to see a lot of her. Didn't like a bloke she got to know.'

'And she just went away, without saying anything?'

'Yeah.'

Checking the contents of a big refrigerator, the other woman considered the matter, wiping her hands on a white cloth. 'We don't do things like that, do we? We tell someone. Or write, anyway. Did she take her clothes?'

'I don't know.'

Élise left the café, and put up her umbrella. A walk of about ten minutes brought her to the shabby building where Marie had a 'studio', in reality just a room with plastic curtains dividing off the cooking and washing areas. Élise hadn't been there much: Marie had always preferred to come to her, since she hated the concierge of the building.

Nevertheless, the harpy now recognised Élise as she opened the outer door, and began an outraged tirade. 'Yes, you're her friend, aren't you - and just the same type. She hasn't paid the landlord any rent for this month. I have to look out for her, that's what he said, but where is she, I ask you? Run off with some man, I suppose, like the tart she is. And she owes me ten francs for getting her some groceries, out of the goodness of my heart.'

'Yes, and you probably made a good profit on them. Will you let me into her room?'

'No, I won't - how do I know you won't pinch anything? What she's left behind - he'll take it instead of the rent. Not that it's worth anything, I don't suppose it's more than a heap of rubbish, anyway. I'm not letting you in, anyway, so you can take yourself off. You and that Marie Calvert, you're a real pair!'

'Cow!'

As Élise was turning away, a tall man with red hair arrived at the door, shaking the rain off his coat. Something in his belted white coat, the cut of his hair, even the look in his eye, told her. She could practically smell it on him. Cop.

He blocked the way as she tried to slip past along the pavement.

'What was that about Marie Calvert?' he called to the concierge, who had stuck her head out of the doorway like an enraged puppet.

'This creature and she were friends - well, what do you expect? The Calvert girl has disappeared without paying her rent, so if you're a friend of hers as well, you tell her she's in trouble.'

Audran flipped open his police identification. 'We'll have to find her first!' He caught Élise by the waist as she tried again to sidle away. 'Who are you?'

Reluctantly, Élise gave her name, and when the concierge tried to pull the door shut, Audran inserted his foot to hold it open.

'I know who you are, then, you're the one who reported Marie was missing. I want you to come in and help me.'

'You're not bringing that dirty little tart in here!' The concierge's teeth clicked with self-righteousness.

'Watch your tongue! Mademoiselle Barrau will be kindly assisting the police in this enquiry.' His hand had grasped Élise's mackintosh at the back, where the concierge could not see it. She could feel it, anchoring her firmly. There didn't seem to be much choice.

'Yes, *vielle salope*!' she shrieked. 'So you see, you'll have to let me in, after all.'

At least it was a glorious moment of triumph as she sailed in and preceded Audran up the stairs. The concierge pushed past them and unlocked Marie's door.

It was a small room, and the air was damp. The furniture consisted of a few cheap pieces: an armchair with a mustard-coloured nylon covering, a table with a cloth thrown over it. Next to the single bed was a flimsy melamine wardrobe, and against the opposite wall a dressing table. It was strewn with make-up, several little gold tubes of lipstick lying out of their cases.

The room was clean enough, but there was an unpleasant stale smell. Pulling back a flowered plastic curtain, Audran exposed a shower and wash-basin, and lifted up the lid of a wickerwork linen-basket. 'She didn't do her washing before she left, anyway. Look, I want you to go through her clothes and stuff - see what she's taken with her.'

Élise was suddenly serious. The sight of her friend's things, of an old pair of high-heeled shoes kicked off that lay under the table, of the untidy make-up, seemed to bring Marie right into the room, almost as if she were there, trying out the lipsticks, leaning over to see her face in the mirror. 'I don't know - I can't be sure.'

She opened the wardrobe door and saw the blue and white dress. Reaching out her hand, she reluctantly touched it, as if to assure herself of its presence.

'This was her favourite dress. It was new.'

The policeman turned to face her and she saw something surprising, a seriousness, a compassion. He was quite young, after all. 'Just look around, and then I'll take you home,' he said, gently, and she realised that tears were running down her cheeks. Strange, she hadn't realised she was crying till she saw his face.

She dabbed at her cheeks, and, to take her mind off the sad little room, went to the window and looked out. There was a chestnut tree outside, its dripping branches obscuring the light, and she thought of something, about a view from a window.

'The place he took her to. The cottage, or whatever it was.'

'Please tell me.'

'Marie said she saw horses and riders in the distance, from an upstairs window. I just remembered.'

Chapter Forty-five

Marina looked through the window when she was told, into the next room, though Halley had been afraid that she wouldn't be able to go through with it. She'd been in such a state when they brought her to the station, yet there had been a kind of bravery about her determination.

'I know it was very wrong, Inspector,' Professor Sanderson had said, 'It was wrong of us all. Please don't blame Marina too much.'

'Well, wiser heads seem to be deeply implicated!' he had responded sharply. 'Academic status doesn't cut much ice with me, I'm afraid.' But he was well aware of the influence it had on his seniors, and the connections Oxford dons had with the corridors of power. He knew perfectly well, as any realistic and ambitious officer must, that whatever anyone says, the police in Britain are under political control; their policies are ultimately those of the Home Secretary of the day.

'Quite right, Inspector,' said Susan Sanderson. 'I thought I was acting for the best, but as things have turned out, it has just caused more unhappiness. I didn't really anticipate the consequences.'

Among the consequences, Halley reflected grimly to himself, was this terrified girl trying to be brave, as she peered through a one-way window in Thames Valley police headquarters at Kidlington. A woman police officer stood close behind, in case she needed some physical support, as well as the moral kind.

But she managed to say quite clearly, 'Yes, that's him!' as she peered at the row of men.

'What number?'

'Number five. At the end on the right.'

A stocky man, red-faced, unremarkable but for the heavily muscled forearms, unless you saw cruelty in the narrow eyes that darted about unnervingly.

'Who is it again? I'm sorry, but I have to ask you to be clear about this.'

'That is the man I saw in our flat in Woodstock.'

'Please state, for the record, whether you have seen this man anywhere else.'

'Yes.'

Her voice had dropped to almost a whisper, but it was perfectly audible. There was no sound in the room as she spoke.

'It was the man I saw in the grounds of Versailles. I mean, I saw two men. This one was the attacker.'

The identity parade was not dismissed, as was usual. Instead, as the row of men stood before the viewing window, Marina was led out, and another young woman took her place, thin and anxious-looking, but with a greater reserve of calm, almost of stoicism, in her dark eyes. There was somebody else with her, a young man.

'Is this the interpreter?'

'Yes, Inspector.'

'Right. Please ask her if she recognises any of these men.'

There was a rapid exchange, and then the interpreter's voice, formal, uninflected with emotion. One can't tell anything extra, this way, thought Halley. All the little clues that come from the feeling in the way someone says something - I can't read them at second-hand. But what the interpreter was saying was enough, anyway.

'She sees the man who attacked her at Woodstock. The man she tried to escape from in the grounds of Blenheim Palace.'

'Which number in the line-up?

The answer came a moment later.

'Number five.'

Chapter Forty-six

Luke Elmer faced Halley across the table. Noises filtered occasionally into the cell: doors clanging, voices calling out, now shouting, now pleading. The tiny room smelt of piss and disinfectant. The tape was running, the persons present had been duly identified. Formalities on the surface; underneath, a web of tensions, of recalcitrance, of sizing up the odds.

'My client wishes to give the police the fullest possible assistance.' It was the woman lawyer, her hair done up in an untidy bun.

Elmer looked white, twisting his hands. Between the devil and the deep blue sea, thought Halley. And I suppose he's decided we are the lesser of two evils.

They got a name out of him.

'He's known as Vitek. Don't know whether that's his Christian name or his surname. I think he's Slovakian. Brings over Romanies, anyway.'

'What happens on the other side of the Channel?'

'They're brought in through a southern French port - one of the small places, along the Riviera. Then there's a van and they're taken north. Shut in all the time, of course. Eventually there's a transfer to a boat at night.'

'And what happened at Versailles?'

Luke Elmer looked at his lawyer. She seemed to give a slight nod, but he was still reluctant.

'Marina insisted on going on that research trip - she said it would do her a lot of good - let her get away from everything.'

'And in fact precisely the opposite happened, didn't it? By design?'

'I was afraid that - that what she saw in England - that it would be taken seriously. I warned them about it.'

'You warned them - you knew what the consequences might be!'

The woman spoke. 'Inspector, I object to that tone. My client is cooperating fully,'

Halley leaned back in his chair. There was a long pause, while he pushed away the thought, 'You bastard, you wanted her sorted out,' and his mind cooled down.

Elmer was drumming his heels under the desk.

'I never thought - I didn't think - After all, they didn't -'

'Kill her - is that what they might have done?'

The lawyer and her client spoke almost at once - he started up in his chair and said posturingly, 'I told them I wouldn't stand for anything that would hurt her. He didn't mean to kill her at Woodstock - she ran out into the road.'

'Inspector, I must defend my client from these theoretical attacks!'

Halley brought himself to look at the young man as dispassionately as he could. Did this young wimp really think he had been in a position to bargain with the sort of people he'd got involved with?

'You didn't think it would harm her - to be dismissed as a madwoman?'

'Very well - what was it - they tried to destabilise her? Was that it? They wanted her written off as a hysteric, who went round imagining things at historic places? So they put up some sort of show - some kind of charade. You told them when she would be at Versailles and where she was staying, so finding her would have been no trouble at all, would it?'

'But I didn't think they would - not go so far with it.'

The boy's nervous drumming seemed to have spread to his legs now - his body seemed to be shaking.

'They put on a performance specially for her?'

Elmer had changed. He suddenly looked terrified, vulnerable.

'I'll tell you what happened.'

The voice was a whisper.

Chapter Forty-seven

'Do you know how the canary trick is done?'

'The canary trick?'

Cecile, sitting opposite Halley in his St. Aldate's office, was uncertain whether she had heard aright.

'Yes - you know, the magician, with the little yellow bird? They have them in France too, I suppose?'

'Yes - of course, I know what you mean.' She recalled scenes from old movies, old posters, men with tall shiny hats and twirling capes. 'But I've never actually seen it done on the stage.'

'No, neither have I - but it used to be a famous music hall act. The conjuror has a live bird, a canary - there's no doubt it's alive, the audience sees it fluttering about in a cage. Then he whisks the top hat off his head, pops the bird in it, puts something over the hat - a board, say - so the bird can't fly out. Then he collapses the hat - boom!' and Halley slammed his clenched fist on the desk.

'It goes down like a concertina. Flat as a pancake! The magician murmurs a few words of mumbo-jumbo, "abracadabra" and so on, passes his wand back and forth over the hat. Then he shows the inside of the hat to the audience. And, hey, presto! It's empty! No canary fluttering inside - nothing but the silk lining of the hat! The audience is gasping - where's the bird gone? Then the conjuror opens his hand - and lo and behold, the bird flutters out quite unharmed and flies off happily.'

Cecile was leaning forward, listening carefully. 'And how is it done, this trick? Is there some secret way the bird is concealed inside the hat all the time, before it flies out?'

'No - there wouldn't be room at the bottom of the hat for a bird fluttering about. Think again.'

She laughed. 'You know, it must be one of the oldest illusions around, I suppose - but I've no idea how it's done. How the bird disappears and re-appears.'

'Nor do most of us, madame, because we want to believe - and most human beings don't want to know the truth!'

'The truth?'

'Yes, people don't think of it, because it's not pleasant. There you are, being entertained, sitting in the theatre, you're having a happy evening out, the conjuror is friendly, a genial fellow, the type you'd trust your little children with ...'

'So what is it - come on, don't keep me in suspense.'

'How much do you think the life of a canary is worth?'

'Very little, I imagine. '

'Exactly.'

He sat back and Cecile contemplated what he had just said. There was a growing expression of rather fearful anticipation on her face.

'Go on, tell me exactly how it's done.'

'It's quite simple - it's just that the audience never guess. They don't want to know, you see.'

'He just ... disposes ...'

'Exactly! He crushes the hat down with his fist and kills the bird with one blow. Smashes it flat. They're really very tiny, you know. Under the feathers, there's nothing to them - it would all compact into a very small space. There's a false lining inside the hat that slides across and hides the dead bird.'

'And the canary that flies off ...'

'Is another one, produced from the conjuror's sleeve. But it works. You see, it's not an illusion. It's reality. But the audience wants to believe it's a trick - they'd rather believe in magic than that the canary was killed before their eyes, and as for the birds - who will care anyway?'

She stared across the desk, understanding now what Halley was getting at.

'As for the canaries,' she said slowly, carefully, 'Their lives are of no account.'

Chapter Forty-eight

The sun was coming through the narrow windows and Cecile took her pile of books from the young man at the Reserve Desk and walked towards her seat. She slid in between the ancient wooden shelves, and contemplated her surroundings for a few moments, letting the sheer pleasure of the old reading room, its magnificent qualities as a time-machine for scholarship, wash over her. Above was an oak-beamed roof beneath which still stood the bookcases of Duke Humphrey's Library, the oldest part of the Bodleian, muffling all noise, protecting books and readers from the outside world as they had done for centuries. Lining the shelves were tier upon tier of vellum and leather-bound books, which had once been chained here. Through the window to her right was a garden, where she could see a group of young people sitting on benches, their faces animated as they talked with student urgency and feeling.

It had been a wonderful time, when she had herself been a student in Bordeaux, at the magistrates' college, along with other idealists, who were going to change the world. 'We are France's ultimate defence against corruption!' Yes, they had believed that, and there was indeed a new generation of *juges d'instruction,* not compliant with the old order, not afraid of politicians, nor burdened with social deference. And some of them had done great things, and brought down powerful people, simply because a determined examining magistrate could use their powers to impound evidence, to pursue allegations of bribery, and take the battle right into the very houses of France's most autocratic ministers.

'We have not entirely lost our ideals,' she said to herself. 'We are achieving something.' In her heart of hearts, she utterly despised those cynics who asked whether any new generation of idealists did not become embittered by experience. 'No,' she thought, 'because there is always a new battle to fight.'

She turned from the young faces in the garden to the books in front of her, graded in a neat pile. The first was a tiny thing, bound in worn walnut-brown leather. Inside the front cover someone had once practised writing in French with a shaky quill pen. The misspelled single word straggling uncertainly across at the top was oddly chosen. Cecile read it with a start of surprise: *'acusateur.'* Beside it was written a date, 'Febry 22nd, 1782. Owen.' What accuser? Who had preoccupied the mind of the owner, one Owen, more than two centuries ago, so that the hand felt compelled to trace it across a book?

She opened the first page and studied the title. *'L'esprit familier du Trianon. L'apparition de la Duchesse de Fontange contenant les secrets de ses Amours, les particularités de son empoisonnement et de sa Mort.'* She noted down an English translation for future reference: 'The ghost of the Trianon. The apparition of the Duchess of Fontanges, containing the secret of her loves, the details of her poisoning and her death.'

This was the Grand Trianon, it seemed, where Louis XIV had created a love-nest for his mistress, the Duchesse., in the grounds of the Château. There was a frontispiece with an appropriate decoration: an apparition appearing at the side of a bed in the form of a woman, naked to the waist, her cloak thrown back over her shoulders to expose her full breasts. She was pulling back the curtains of a bed where a figure in a night-cap was starting up in alarm.

Cecile began to read: The Trianon, it appeared, was considered the most enchanted spot of all the royal pleasure grounds, and as her eyes moved over the small pages, concentrating on the old print, she began to realise it was a work of erotica, discreet, but voluptuous, that Owen - was this his first name or second? - had possessed in the early spring of 1782, when Marie -Antoinette was still alive, and instructing her architect, Richard Mique, in the pleasure gardens of Versailles. It had already been an old book, perhaps passed down from one young English gentleman to another. 'Something spicy here - the best way to learn French, I assure you!'

According to this work the Trianon had been built by Louis for La Fontange, and furnished accordingly. 'The King followed the inclination of his favourite mistress by preferring it to Versailles. He created an angel's bed, the 'sky' made from Venetian mirror glass.

When one lifted the curtains, it was surrounded by other mirrors. The sheets were black taffeta so that the skin of the mistress might appear more white. In this same bed he saw the Apparition.'

It appeared that the King's regular mistress, perhaps his wife, Madame de Montespan, became jealous of the young and beautiful favourite. She sent her rival a bouillon into which she had dropped a poisonous powder, and the poor Duchess died in agony.

One night on the feast of his patron saint, Saint Louis, the King wanted to sleep in that bed at the Trianon with the Montespan, who told him that she had long renounced 'the pleasures of Venus'. But he persisted, and she gave way, and, after several bouts of love-making, he fell asleep, to be roused when the bed-curtains were pulled back, by the spirit of the Duchess, who accused her rival of murder. Numerous detailed tales of the debauchery of the French court were then recounted by the avenging apparition, and the King was begged to reform.

Erotica lightly disguised as a moral fable, thought Cecile with some amusement. The 'acusateur' was presumably the ghost of the Duchess herself. Still, it seemed an odd word to pick out of the book and write down. What had been the impulse to do so, on that February day in 1782?

What was of more immediate interest was another question. She went to the staff desk and put her enquiry, and after a minute or two a friendly fellow with heavy eyebrows bustled over to where she had been sitting and picked up the little book.

'Oh, yes, this is from one of our old collections,' he said, knowledgeably. 'It would most certainly have been in the library in 1900. Anyone looking at the old catalogue - we had a series of huge volumes with entries for books pasted in on slips of paper - anyone looking under "Versailles" would have found it.'

'Thank you very much,' said Cecile.

Chapter Forty-nine

'I believe they didn't see anything,' said Marina. 'At least, only with the eye of hallucination.'

'Wasn't there supposed to be some evidence? There was the map that was found afterwards in an old chimney,' said Professor Sanderson. 'The map showed the little temple and a ravine, as they claim in their book, didn't it? That became a famous part of the evidence. They had seen something that no one knew about - until the original plans for the gardens of the Petit Trianon were discovered.'

'Yes - Mique's map of the grounds of Versailles. He was the architect employed to design the grounds. The map is well known - there must have been many copies circulating in the eighteenth century, and it's a very confused document - very difficult, actually, to make out the features they had seen.'

'In any case,' said Cecile, leaning forward, following the discussion carefully, 'there is a considerable failure of logic, isn't there?'

The two women turned towards her. They were all three comfortably seated in the little back bar of The King's Arms, glasses of wine and mineral water set out respectively before Marina and Susan Sanderson, and a half-pint of the local Hook Norton beer, recommended for *le goût du pays*, in front of Cecile.

'They can't have it both ways,' Cecile continued. 'If they stepped back in time and saw things as they actually were, how could they see the original projects for the gardens? Things that had never been built. As I understand it, Marie-Antoinette's architects, Gabriel and Mique, and the gardeners, Richard *père et fils*, came up with numerous schemes - they even presented her with small models of the temples and so on. So if Eleanor Jourdain and Annie Moberly claimed to have walked back into history, why would they see things that hadn't been created? And their book, 'An Adventure', doesn't give any specific references as to the whereabouts of this map after it had been found up the chimney of an old house in Montmorency, or tell us which library it was in when Eleanor saw it.

They just said the map was in a library in Versailles. I asked my husband to check. Daniel phoned from France last night. There is no such map in the public library at Versailles, which inherited the library of the Château of Versailles after the Revolution.'

'There seems no independent evidence for the chimney story,' agreed Marina. 'I think Eleanor Jourdain was inclined to believe any romantic bits and pieces she was told. She wasn't very scrupulous with the truth, you know. Mique's plans for the grounds were found, quite surprisingly, but they weren't in any romantic old chimney. They weren't even in a house in Montmorency, near Paris. They were in a red leather folder in a library at Modena in Italy, along with sketches and watercolours of the Petit Trianon and its surroundings. The Archduke Ferdinand, Governor of Lombardy visited Versailles in 1786, and he was married to a woman of the Este clan, so the folder ended up in her family library. And its contents were described in print by Pierre de Nolhac, one of the leading authorities on Versailles. I think Jourdain filled her head with a lot of silly legends she found in books, and even made some up.'

'Oh, I always thought she was a real academic,' said Professor Sanderson, sipping her wine thoughtfully. A throng of tourists went past the window of the little bar, and Marina paused for a moment for the hubbub to die down before she went on.

'Miss Jourdain wasn't a very good researcher. For example, they naturally investigated the question of whether a film was being made in the grounds that day, or whether a fête was being photographed, or something of that sort. Pathé had made a film about Marie-Antoinette, but in January, 1910. There was a record book kept at the Château, which showed no sign of permission being given for any filming or any similar event in August, 1901, and Eleanor Jourdain says "it was placed before me" so that she could verify that. But the record book wasn't placed before her, she actually sneaked a look at it without the permission of the authorities. That's in a letter to Miss Moberly.'

'But it doesn't make any real difference to the truth of the story, if there was no actual record of film-making,' pointed out the Professor.

'No, that's not quite true,' said Cecile suddenly, with a lot of feeling, so that the other two looked at her in surprise. She went on, struggling a bit with the concepts she was trying to get across in a foreign language. 'It makes a difference as to how you regard her veracity. She was not a very scrupulous person, I think.'

'No, she wasn't,' said Marina. 'In fact, she was an unattractive person, in many ways. Apparently she used to sneak around St. Hugh's College in slippers, listening at the students' doors.'

'An all-women college?' asked Cecile, who had noticed that there were men going in and out of the colleges which she had supposed to be reserved for women.

'Oh, yes, none of them were mixed at that time. And she had her favourites, apparently.'

'Did she have any other experiences - like the one in Versailles?'

'Yes. She told her students she had seen a gallows - at the end of the Woodstock Road, here in Oxford. I don't think anyone took that seriously. The point about the Versailles experience was that two people underwent it, confirming each other.'

'But, looking carefully at the evidence,' Cecile pursued her point,' they saw different things. And the most striking thing is that they appear to have told no one else at the time - you'd think the natural thing would be to rush out and tell the world of such an extraordinary event.'

'And they did that - but ten years later!' agreed Marina. 'I think they'd been talking about it to their acquaintances, maybe embroidering and adding to it over the years - and in the end they were forced to come out in the open and defend it.'

'And to hide certain things,' said Cecile. 'You noticed that, too?'

'The Ménégoz business?' Marina turned to Professor Sanderson, who was looking puzzled. 'Mademoiselle Ménégoz was the French mistress at Eleanor's school at Watford - she was a close friend, and a business partner in the school venture. And when they went to Paris for that visit in the August of 1901, it was in an apartment belonging to the Ménégoz family that they stayed, on the Boulevard Raspail. And later in that year, in November, Jeanne Ménégoz told Moberly and Jourdain about legends that the ghost of

Marie-Antoinette haunted the Trianon. But that was after their experiences there.'

'Their alleged experiences,' put in Cecile.

'Something happened to them, even if it wasn't a visitation from ghosts.'

'Yes, I accept that. But the strange thing is this: they appear to have said nothing to Jeanne Ménégoz about the Trianon affair for over three months - now, wouldn't it have been the natural thing for her to have been one of the first people they spoke to? After all, she was herself French and familiar with all the history of the place? Eleanor Jourdain didn't say anything about the ghostly apparitions till later in November, 1901, after Jeanne Ménégoz had repeated some old stories about Versailles, of Marie-Antoinette and her courtiers manifesting themselves at the Petit Trianon. She said it was just a tradition. She had been told that the Queen and her friends had been seen dancing near there on summer evenings, a century after they had been victims of the guillotine.'

'Yes, I think those stories could be dismissed as gossip and legend - they were very vague. 'But you saw what had happened to the notebook?' asked Marina.

'I did. The name of Ménégoz has been blanked out everywhere. I could just make it out occasionally, looking at the reverse side of the pages on which it appeared. It showed through the paper in a few places. But someone went to great trouble to try and make sure no one could read it. It was covered up. All we have left is "Mlle. M."

'And very carefully concealed not just scribbled out, but with white stamp-paper stuck all over it, wherever the name occurred.'

'Which suggests it was done quite unofficially, not by St. Hugh's College nor by the Library, but by the woman who bequeathed the notebooks to the Bodleian - Annie Moberly herself,' commented the Professor.

'And if we ask why she should do such a thing,' Marina took up the point, 'then look at all the names in those notebooks - all the people who testified that Miss Moberly and Miss Jourdain had spoken to them of the incident soon after it occurred. All of them - but the one person whom one might have expected them to confide in, the woman closest to the whole adventure - her name has been blanked out!'

'What does that suggest to you?' asked Cecile, carefully.

Marina reflected. 'I've been turning and turning this over in my mind,' she said eventually. 'I think Jeanne Ménégoz didn't believe them. I think she refused to support their story. And Annie Moberly was desperate no one should know that. Because if Jeanne Ménégoz, Eleanor's Jourdain's close friend, her business partner, a Frenchwoman conversant with all the stories about Versailles, didn't believe them, then why should anyone else?'

'Those two were stranger characters than one might think, I have the impression.' Cecile felt that perhaps she was prompting the girl too much, but Marina gave a thoughtful response.

'Eleanor Jourdain in particular seems to have been of a very fanciful disposition and not nearly so knowledgeable about France as she made out. She had a terrible French accent, apparently. Their chief virtue was their respectability, I think.'

'That must have taken a terrible battering at Versailles!'

'Yes,' said Marina, recalling the lush statuary, the paintings, the whole erotic atmosphere with which the place was charged. 'It's full of half-naked nymphs and gods - and of course, it's all made quite plain and open there, about Louis' mistresses. The rooms in which they lived so that he could visit them discreetly and so on. Must have been quite a shock for two Victorian spinsters. Sex is so much on show for us, we barely notice it - but then, it must have been quite different. After all, Versailles just oozes sexuality. There were these two strait-laced Victorian women, wandering along on a hot summer's day, going round the Château with all the stories about the royal bedfellows, and then walking out in the grounds, and seeing all those sculptures with just a few wisps of clothing round their loins - of course, we're so used to nakedness now, but that was an era which was so prudish they covered everything up frantically. The grounds of Versailles, the nude river-gods in the fountains, bronze ladies with their breasts hanging out of their *corsages* - how dreadful they must have seemed. Moberly and Jourdain had probably never been exposed to anything like it.'

'It seems to me,' said Cecile, taking a sip of her beer, 'that Versailles has always had a certain erotic focus for the English. Look at that little book in the Bodleian - about the King's mistresses at the Trianon. It's something the French have always been quite open about - but I don't think two English ladies would have regarded it in the same light. It's part of the myth of France for British people - sex and frivolity. Perhaps we can try and get a bit closer to the truth. I say to myself, "Here are two intelligent women. They wouldn't keep up a fantasy."

And she looked across the table at Susan Sanderson and Marina Cassatt.

Chapter Fifty

Audran got back wearily, but there were at least three more establishments to contact. He had got used to the drill by now, the curious heads poking out, the clattering hooves, the grooms preoccupied with their charges. In wet weather, it was even worse - the steam that came off the animals, and the wet heaps in the yards, all seemed to exude a smell that clung to him.

'No, never seen anywhere like that. Yes, we take the string out every day.'

When he thought about Élise's mention of the horses which Marie had glimpsed in the distance, Audran's heart had sunk into his boots.

'Horses, she says? God, this place is surrounded by them - stables, riding-schools, horse trainers.'

'Apparently Marie mentioned she had seen horses passing nearby. That's the only thing that gives us any location so far.'

'No!' replied Colas, the next morning. 'You have to get to this - the report's just come in.' He lifted his hand in an angry gesture and banged it down. 'There is no other possibility - I'm not having my officers chasing off after any false trails that *madame le juge* cares to set up in her whims. I've no doubt this fellow the Calvert woman took up with is a rotten bastard, but I'm deciding priorities here - understood?'

Audran slapped his gloved hands together and moved reluctantly away from his boss. He knew it would be useless to argue. Colas' rage would be terrible enough when he discovered Audran had got two junior men going round trying to track down Toni's 'country retreat'. It was pretty hit and miss since they had lost the man himself: Audran knew that the only chance of success in the search for Marie was now the dead grind, the painstaking enquiries, the meticulous searching for some odd unpatterned events, unexplained activities in the regions where the suspect had his interests. A nosy neighbour, that unvalued pearl so often encountered in the heart of the French countryside? Maybe the rural retreat was out of sight, out of earshot. The string of horses was the best lead they had, so far. Versailles was essentially suburban in character, yet the vast extent of the Château grounds before the revolution had left the district still retaining huge stretches of parkland and woods outside the official bounds of the Château. As for the grounds themselves - the surrounding wall was forty-three kilometres long, and there were no less than twenty-two entrances - figures he had received from the Château authorities, along with an assortment of maps and plans. Searching the whole vast extent would take utterly disproportionate totals of man-hours. In a sense, Audran acknowledged that Colas had right on his side. He had to justify his utilisation of police resources, after all.

Fifteen minutes later, Audran contemplated the sun shining down a narrow alleyway. Other figures busied themselves in the light of day, and the relentless humming of the Paris trains and station announcements came from behind a high wall as a constant accompaniment.

This was a narrow cul-de-sac next to the Rive Droite station, running parallel with one of the elegant tree-lined boulevards, at the backs of the houses. It was rarely used, except in the morning and evening rush-hours, when commuters used it as a short-cut to the station, accessible through a flight of steps. Otherwise, it was undisturbed, except for the occasional traveller hurrying along.

It was one of these, a well-dressed middle-aged woman, who stood now to one side, beyond a protective cordon sealing off the top of the alley. She was holding a handkerchief to her weeping face, supported by a policewoman who held her arm.

Further down, a stretcher was being lifted out of a police ambulance and beyond lay a long, white-shrouded shape. The scene was easy enough to reconstruct: the body, the discoverer, the authorities duly summoned.

Audran walked through the barrier set up at the entrance to the alley, flipping open his identification towards the policeman on duty. He gave the woman a glance as he passed, noting the expensive clothes and well-cut grey hair and assessing her automatically as a wealthy wife going to spend a day shopping in Paris. Not the sort of woman who otherwise would ever have walked through an alleyway.

The body had been rolled beneath some bushes, which partly covered it. As Audran watched, the medics finished their work, and signalled for the stretcher. The face could not be seen: the long hair had tumbled over it, and this had been a blessing for the woman whose fine leather court shoes had stumbled in the blood around the body.

He started back down the alleyway, leaving two men to search the area, and despatched another to the station, to ask whether the staff had heard or seen anything. It was unlikely: there was a constant stream of tourists passing through the station, and the shunting and banging of the trains would have masked almost any noise - even a gunshot. The alleyway was a well-chosen spot for a killing. But that was jumping to conclusions: the murder had not necessarily taken place there, he reminded himself. Better wait for the pathologist's findings before jumping to conclusions.

He moved towards the weeping woman; an official statement would be needed. There'd be a *juge d'instruction* on the case, of course - as yet, he didn't know who, someone who would have had to shoulder part of Cecile's work-load in addition to their own, no doubt, and would be thoroughly pissed off as a result.

An hour later, he was sitting with Colas outside the morgue. Locard came out, rubbing his back wearily. 'I've dictated the official report,'he told Colas, who was in the back of the gleaming black Peugeot.

'Give me a summary.'

Locard was accustomed to the police inspector's tone. He'd complained about it before, officially and unofficially - 'lack of professional respect ... intimidating manner ...' but it hadn't done much good. Colas, Locard had decided, was just a crass bastard by nature.

All the same, there was some unexpected anxiety about the man today.

'Well, death was due to a gunshot wound in the head, just above the left ear. Very efficient. Not a rage killing, not a brawl.'

'What can you tell us about the victim?'

'Young, thin, long fair hair, no overt marks or scars. More after the post-mortem. There is something odd, though. Well, a couple of things.'

Locard was deliberately irritating Colas, thought Audran, with some pleasure.

'The first - there seem to be traces of some white powder in the hair.'

'Drugs? Weird!'

'We'll get it analysed. And, as I said, there were two other strange things.'

'Get on with it! The sooner you tell us, the sooner we can try to get her identified.'

Locard laughed in a curious fashion.

'Well, the other point is that someone already had a go, quite recently. There were light bruises on the neck.'

The pathologist held out his hands, curved in the air as if they were gripping an invisible neck.

'I'd say the marks were a few days old. Not enough pressure was used to break anything, no crushing injuries. Strange - it looked as though the force that was used hadn't really been intended to do any harm. It wasn't a serious attack, just enough to leave marks on the skin, that was all. But then, later on, someone used violence in earnest. With a gun.'

'Looks like your hunt is off, anyway,' said Colas to Audran.

There was a pause. Could be, Audran thought. If Toni had been brutal with her, and that violence had then escalated. Some people played sex-games involving more brutality than the pathologist had described as having been applied on the neck of the victim.

But he'd never come across a case where domestic or sexual violence ended in such a shooting, not this neat, professional sort of killing, anyway. There were the family hostage crises, of course, where some idiot waved a gun around, and terrified neighbours called the police eventually. Usually, it was some paranoid schizo who believed his wife or his girlfriend was cheating on him. But this murder: one neat bullet-hole drilled in the skull, the body placed in an alleyway where the chances were it wouldn't be spotted for some time, where the killer could make a quick get-away from the station, furthermore. All this added up to some cool and careful forethought. Was Toni really that kind of a murderer?

'Well, the sooner we can get a description out, the sooner we stand a chance of identifying her,' said Colas.

Locard looked like a cat that had got at the cream. A great beam came over his face, and with a theatrical geniality he said;

'Her? It was a male. I assure you, there's no doubt about that!'

Chapter Fifty-one

'I don't know where the hell you start,' Audran said to himself. 'Horses, horses, don't know anything about the beasts. All those posh riding-schools.'

'Just one more morning,' he eventually found himself muttering aloud. Colas had reluctantly extended the deadline, after a long phone call from England.

'You damned peasant from the *gendarmerie*!' he had said to Audran. 'Can't you at least get the sex right?'

Audran had rightly interpreted this to mean, 'You made me look a fool.'

'All right, I just went by the long hair. And the silky shirt, as well. Anyone could be forgiven - and it didn't matter. After all. It was only for a few minutes we thought it was a woman.'

'Thought it was *the* woman, Marie? What's her name?'

'Calvert. No, she's still missing. Chief, can I continue the search for her?'

Colas looked at him nastily. 'No! Bloody hell, I can't extend the deadline!'

Audran picked his next words carefully. 'Madame Galant thought there was something in the English girl's story, the one who claimed to have seen the murder in the grounds of the Château.'

'So? What's that got to do with it?'

'So she was right. And she might be right about the Calvert woman, too.'

'There's no proof she's missing.'

'Élise Barrau thinks that she hadn't packed any clothes, if she left voluntarily.'

'Barrau? That dyed blonde slut, hair like brass. They'll say anything, do anything for drink or drugs.'

Audran stared at the wall after Colas had put down the phone, recalling warm meshes of harsh yellow hair on a pillow. He must have been a complete fool to go to bed with her, yet something within him rebelled against this summary dismissal of the night he had spent with Élise Barrau. It would wreck his career if it ever came out, and make him a laughing-stock as well, having sex with a woman like that. But he didn't regret it, found himself even wanting her again.

He forced his mind back to the professional problems. Colas had given him one more day. In any case, they would need time, to get some evidence translated into French, including the Romanian documents found in the long-haired boy's pocket and the statement in English made by Luke Elmer in Oxford.

The following morning, Audran was still working his way through the listing of riding-schools and stables near Versailles, systematically ticking them off. He'd found the 'Centre Hippique', out at Marnes, on the edge of the remaining forest areas around Thierry and La Porte Verte, and started there. At first he had thought he could just make his enquiries sitting in his office and ringing the places up, but he soon realised that was pretty useless, because the people he needed to really speak to, the jockeys or stable-boys or trainers who actually went out with the horses, were usually with their charges and not hanging around the offices. His own hunting-ground was too vast, an open space that had once been reserved for the royal chase, and was now a public park where long paths ran between the remains of old forests.

It was a grey, drizzly day and he turned up the collar of his coat as he got out of the car in front of the third stables that morning. The cobbled yard was slippery. He put the questions to the first person he encountered, a woman in breeches, weather-beaten yet still handsome, the eyes bright cornflower blue in the tanned face.

He put the question yet again. Was there any old neglected building on the route they took when they were exercising the horses, and if so had they noticed anything strange?

It was a chance in ten thousand, he thought to himself, now as every previous time, but kept his face impassive. Last day, anyway. Colas wouldn't let him carry on with it any longer, he was sure of that.

'No, there wasn't anything I noticed - but hang on, I don't go out every day. I'll ask the others.'

There were two more of them, Julien and Philippa. The latter was an English girl from Newbury, gaining experience in the French equestrian world.

'It's all old buildings round here.' Her open face stated the obvious truth. 'We go past lots of them every day in the parks - old cottages or lodges. Most of them have been done up, though - I wouldn't say I remember anything that was dilapidated.'

She had some trouble with the French word for it, but Julien seconded her quickly when he worked out what she meant. He was a big lad for a jockey, Audran thought, for he was getting used to stable people. Maybe Julien had grown too heavy for racing. But he was rubbing the velvety nose of a big bay horse with extraordinary gentleness as he spoke to the detective.

'Yes - there are places like that everywhere. I don't recall anything. Well, maybe I did see somewhere a bit tumbledown looking - you can see the chimney through the trees. A small place, maybe an old lodge. But nothing special - just like all the others, really.'

He frowned, as if trying to recollect something, but Audran was giving up and turning away. This was useless. As the English girl said, the whole area was dotted with places that would correspond to that vaguest of descriptions they had from Élise Barrau- a small old place, nothing modernised, surrounded by trees.

Julien called after him, 'There was something. When we went past that place.'

Audran turned back, his feet slipping on the wet stones.

'What was it - did you notice something?'

'Not me. I didn't. But Chevalier did.'

'Chevalier?'

The big bay turned his head, as if answering to his name, and Julien went on to explain.

'We were galloping past - and he suddenly checked and pricked up his ears. I've never known him do that before. It was as if he heard something. I couldn't hear a sound, but their hearing is very acute. Do you know how they trained horses for that circus trick in the old days - the 'Clever Horse' - you know, where the trainer asks the horse the answer to a sum - say three plus four - and the horse paws the ground seven times with its hoof? The trainer clicks the nails of his finger and thumb together - the slightest of sounds, but the horse can hear it, though of course the audience can't. The animal's taught to respond to each tiny click. Don't know why anyone ever shouts at a horse. They can hear a whisper a mile off.'

'When was it you took Chevalier out?'

Julien considered. 'Maybe yesterday or the day before - I'm not exactly sure.'

'Could you take me to the place?' And then, as Julien moved towards the imposing bulk of Chevalier he added hastily, 'No, not on horseback.'

Chapter Fifty-two

Another prison, another country. This man was red-faced, blustering at being made to remain standing in the row. 'Shut the fuck up and get into line!' said a uniformed policeman, economically.

The interpreter translated to the girl on the other side of the window, where Halley was talking to her. 'Don't worry, Elisaveta, he can't see you. Please tell us what you know about this man you have identified.'

'His name is Vitek. He brought us - a group of us - to this country - he arranged it all. He was in the van that went near the park ...'

'Tell us exactly what happened.'

'I've told you so many times!'

'This is a formal identity parade. You must say it again, please.'

The girl stopped and looked down at the floor. Her thin mouth was quivering, as though she was unable to speak. 'Can I have some water?'

A woman police officer brought her a paper cup of water from a cooler. She took a sip and steadied.

'That is the man who tried to rape me in the front of the van. I ran into the park ... and he got hold of me and dragged me back - but at least he pushed me into the back with the others. There was a girl ... I ran towards her, but he pulled me away. Maybe that's why he let me get into the back of the van. The girl ran into the road after me - he jumped in, started the engine, got the van moving, and then he hit her. He drove on! He just drove on! Maybe that's why he forgot to lock the doors.'

The man whom Elisaveta had picked out was formally charged. 'Illegal immigration! You haven't got any evidence - no one would give evidence against me!'

'Conspiring to assist illegal immigration is not the only charge.' Halley's voice was cold, objective.

'You are also charged with attempted rape.'

And, as the man started yelling indignantly, 'We have the witness, we know her name, and we have her evidence. And she'll also testify that you deliberately drove at Marina Cassatt as she lay helpless in the road. I can bring enough charges against you to keep you banged up till you're screaming at the walls.'

Doors clanged behind Halley and the shouting died away as he returned to where Cecile was standing in the interview room from which the girl had observed the identity parade.

'How did you find her, madame? What made you think there was someone hidden in Professor Sanderson's rooms?'

'I didn't. I guessed part of the story, that Professor Sanderson was sure that Marina wasn't fantasising about the incident in the grounds of Blenheim Palace. But that meant that Marina had actually seen someone. In that case, why didn't Professor Sanderson say so, and vindicate the sanity of one of her best students? There must have been something about the girl Marina had seen that had to be kept a secret. So the first question was: What had become of that girl? Where was she?'

'She gave us the rest of the story herself,' said Halley. 'When the van-load of refugees got into the town, Elisaveta escaped from Vitek altogether, and walked part of the way, then got a lift for a few more miles, into the centre of Oxford. But then how did Marina get involved again?'

'She saw Elisaveta in a street in Oxford, begging, apparently, and recognised her as the girl who had been trying to run away at Blenheim. Marina saw she was in a terrible state and wanted to do something to help, so she took her to Chancellor's College. They didn't have the heart to take her to the police, and besides, one of the science tutors had actually heard of Elisaveta when she was on a visit to Bucharest, and the college tried to help the girl from then on. Professor Sanderson wanted to give her a new start - apparently she's a very brilliant medical student, and Chancellor's College was willing to give her a place and a scholarship. But of course, she was in the country illegally - the Professor knew that, but she let her stay in the College. She had a spare room on her own - what do they say in these colleges...? - on her own staircase.' Marina knew what had happened - and that she hadn't imagined it. And she knew what would happen to the girl if Vitek got hold of her again. And in a way, the whole thing saved Marina's sanity - it was proof she hadn't imagined it. But she couldn't say anything without giving the girl away. It was a terrible dilemma for her.'

'And the boyfriend had tried to get her dismissed as a crazy.' Halley rubbed his chin thoughfully. 'It would have been too much of a coincidence, that Marina happened to be in the park at the same time as this girl.'

'Yes, it was because Luke was involved in the whole thing - he had gone out to meet Vitek. He told Marina he was going for a walk, and when he was late getting back she went to look for him, remember.'

'What was his involvement?'

'Oh, money. The asylum-seekers - or let's call them refugees, since 'asylum-seekers' seems to be almost a dirty word in this country - need somewhere to stay, even if only overnight, and the department of the council where Luke worked had to give planning permission for hostels and boarding-houses. Apparently Vitek took Luke on his pay-roll - all he had to do was to turn a blind eye to any investigations, and tip Vitek off about any council properties that might be conveniently empty for a while. Luke probably wasn't earning much, and the cost of living round here is phenomenal, isn't it? And Marina wouldn't be getting a job till she finished her thesis. But maybe something else attracted Luke, as well, something that Vitek gets out of it too.'

'What was that?' In reality, the policeman had anticipated her answer.

'It gave them power,' said Cecile. 'Power over helpless people. A very attractive incentive, for some.'

Chapter Fifty-three

Cecile walked into the Bodleian for the last time. 'It shouldn't matter to me,' she told herself.

But it did, because she had a compulsive need to finish things, to take them through to their conclusions. And there was a story that hadn't ended - at least, not to her satisfaction.

Why did Annie Moberly keep those records up with such care - only to drop them completely? They ended in 1924.

Cecile had ordered up copies of something called the 'Oxford Magazine', and here she found the records of a feverish little world, Oxford of the nineteen-twenties. The women's colleges, it seemed, had been treated partly as jokes, partly as threats. At any rate, some people took them seriously.

One of those people was Lord Curzon, the eminent politician who was also Chancellor of the University of Oxford, charged with inquiring into serious academic disputes.

And St. Hugh's College seemed to have taken up a considerable amount of his time. What a quarrelsome lot they seemed to have been, when Miss Jourdain became Principal after Miss Moberly's retirement!

Cecile read on, and with a sense of shock realised why the notes ended suddenly in 1924.

Back in Woodstock, Mrs. Robertson said hastily, when Cecile went down to settle her bill, 'I hope you're not going to pay me in them aykews, or eweros, or whatever they are!'

'I wouldn't dream of attempting to do so,' said Cecile. 'After all, Blenheim Palace is named after the place where your Duke of Marlborough defeated a French army, isn't it?'

Mrs. Robertson had the grace to look ashamed. 'Well, it doesn't matter now, I suppose,' she said. 'These things were all such a long time ago, after all.'

'I think I'll need to buy an umbrella before I next go to Oxford,' said Cecile with a tactful switch of the subject. 'I think I left mine on the bus.'

'It's good of you to accompany me,' she said the next morning, shaking the spare umbrella loaned to her by Mrs. Robertson for this expedition.

'Not at all,' said Susan Sanderson. 'Though I'm afraid we may get some rain.' Her plump figure was swathed in a plastic mackintosh. 'Heavens, I haven't walked around these streets for ages. This is what people mean when they talk about North Oxford - the old Victorian houses and huge gardens.'

'What will happen to Elisaveta?' asked Cecile. 'Can she stay in Oxford?'

'No. She'll have to go back home and start again - but the College has offered her a place and a scholarship to go with it, so she'll get here eventually.'

'Good. I hate the way those people are treated as parasites.'

'I know - but I should have stuck to legal means of getting her to Oxford. She can apply for a student visa - after that, we'll see how the world goes.'

They had walked a little way north of St. Giles, and turned into a road called Norham Gardens. The houses were indeed vast, brick built, with extraordinary magpie architectural details pillaged from everywhere, here a row of Gothic chapel windows, there a classical porch tacked on to Byzantine-style brickwork. 'They were built for married dons, originally - when they were first allowed to take wives, big enough for their huge families and quantities of servants. They're mostly University departments, now.'

'The gardens look very old, too.' Cecile found she disliked this architecture more than she cared to admit. In fact, the intensity of her feelings surprised her. 'How strange,' she thought to herself. 'I believed I was a more rational person, not so affected by my surroundings.'

'Yes, some of these trees must have been here for almost a century and a half, now.'

Huge branches spread over the front gardens, darkening the houses. The brickwork, mostly yellowish, looked damp: the trees seemed to trap the moisture in the heavy air. There were glimpses of rutted brown driveways, long stretches of lawns. Through many of the windows could be seen book-covered walls, much as they would have looked a century ago. The houses were set well back from the roadway, which was in any case almost empty. The only life was provided by a group of Italian teenagers waiting with their luggage outside one of the houses, the boys engaged in some wrestling game.

Cecile had the impression that almost anything could have gone on inside those houses, which oozed a massive suburban respectability and she found herself brooding on all those clever minds which had been confined here and all the twists and complexities of which they must have been capable.

They were turning a corner now. 'This is Fyfield Road,' said Professor Sanderson. Didn't you mention it?'

'Yes, the name of that road was on the death certificate. But it wasn't where the final event occurred. That was in Norham Road.'

Professor Sanderson looked up at the sky and produced a small tartan umbrella from somewhere in the depths of her handbag. 'Norham Road is just over there. That's where they lived.'

More of those vast Victorian piles. Perhaps they hadn't been quite so gloomy, then, when there were children and nursemaids about.

Cecile tried to imagine it. Eleanor Jourdain had been a plump little woman, with neat hands and feet, as appeared by her photographs. She pictured a small figure in a tightly-laced dress, bustling along the street, past the high hedges. It was an image that gave Cecile a most unpleasant sensation.

It was along this sedate suburban street that somebody - a housemaid, perhaps, a gardener? - had run on an April day in 1924, to summon Harry Jourdain from his home in Fyfield Road to his sister's house in the neighbouring street.

'Brother. In attendance.'

In attendance at the death, that meant. It was on the certificate.

For as the University waited for Lord Curzon's report to be made public, Eleanor Jourdain, who must have been already apprised of its contents, died at the home that she and Annie Moberly shared in Norham Road.

'They said it was suicide, of course.' Susan Sanderson was shaking out her umbrella.

'I've seen the death certificate,' said Cecile.'She had coronary heart disease and asthma.'

'Officially, a heart attack, then. But I expect she just couldn't face being found out.'

'But what about Miss Moberly.'

'She lived on for another thirteen years. She went on claiming that every word they had said was the gospel truth. I think she regarded herself as the keeper of the flame, so as to speak, after Eleanor's death.'

'But she didn't record anything more in her notebooks.'

Professor Sanderson stopped in the damp street and looked curiously at her. 'You are very thorough! You'd make a good academic!'

Chapter Fifty-four

'She can come back to the South,' he said to Babette. 'We've dealt with the problem. I can't let her know through official channels.'

Maubourg walked through the glass door and stared out from the tower-block balcony perched high on a hill, with a glimpse of the cranes and docks in the distance, sketched darkly against the evening sky. The city of Marseilles was spread out in the lurid colours of sunset, cooling down after the fierce heat of the day.

Babette came out with a glass of cold lemonade for him.

'Here,' she ordered him. 'Sit down for a bit. You look worn out. All hollow-cheeked!'

They settled down and looked out at Marseilles. The smell of lavender rose from a bunch of old petrol-cans painted white, where Babette grew her herbs on the balcony.

Below them, at the entrance to the blocks, distant figures poured out across the concrete walkways, moving in groups, colliding and edging away in some distant choreography, harmless from these heights.

'They have one thing in common, these gangs,' said Babette. 'Whether they're Algerians, Chechens, whatever, they hate coppers with all their heart and soul. They'd kill you on sight if they knew what you do.'

It wasn't a threat, merely a statement. Babette wasn't much like her daughter, Maubourg thought, not physically, anyway, though sometimes they shared a directness of speech. She was a short, thickset woman, with stiff arms and hips, and her grey-streaked hair was dark brown, unlike Cecile's blonde strands. Her eyes were deep-set, suspicious now, but she looked the sort of woman who enjoyed a good laugh.

She took a sip of the lemonade and said, '*Oh, du pipi de chat!*'

He laughed, and she said, 'If you'll excuse the expression! I didn't put enough sliced lemon peel in it.'

'It's fine.'

'And you're a liar. Of course, I can't tell my neighbours what Cecile does, either. They wouldn't understand that - they'd think she's gone over to the other side. Not much of a place, this, is it? I know I can't really have my granddaughter here for long - it's no environment for a child. Oh, Cecile and Daniel would find me somewhere decent to go, if I wanted it. But these are the people I've lived with all my life, round here. It's a great thing to have someone you can talk to. Really tell things to, I mean.'

'Can't you talk to Cecile?'

'She leads a different life now. She tries, but all the same ...'

Maubourg was silent, trying to think of the cool, elegantly dressed woman he knew as a *juge d'instruction* and to rationalise the image of Cecile Galant with this poverty-stricken, crime-ridden background. 'What was she like when she was younger?' he asked.

Babette looked away, out over the city, avoiding looking at him.

'She was a happy, ordinary girl, I would say. Had plenty of pals, was interested in clothes and make-up, that sort of thing. But then - she had a brother, you see. Guillaume. I was working all the time - I had to, there was no choice, so they'd been left on their own since they were little kids, really. Their father walked out a long time ago, so I was on my own. Anyway, there was Guillaume.'

'Don't tell me if you don't want to talk about it.'

'It's all right. I've been over it again and again. Guillaume got mixed up with drugs. He was ... selling stuff. I don't know what - I never know what they're doing, those boys down there. He was fourteen. I'd always gone on about how we needed money ...'

'That wouldn't have been the reason - I promise you.'

'That's what Cecile said. "Maman," she said, "we all have complicated reasons for everything, even if we're only fourteen. He wanted a lot out of life, and that's why he did it." That's how she put it - Cecile is always good with words. They found him down there - on one of the walkways. They'd killed him - the suppliers from a rival gang, I think that was the theory. Anyway, it changed Cecile. She became a different person, almost, working at her books all the time, she had a kind of determination that you never see in the kids round here.'

'And that was how she got to college?'

'Yes. Of course, I was so proud of her, but it was how I lost her, too, in a way. You see, once people get away from this kind of life, they never come back - I mean, you'd be mad to, honestly, wouldn't you?'

Babette was looking at him now. There was a kind of directness about this woman - as if she had retained a sort of peasant simplicity, even here in this twentieth-century concrete eyrie. As well as the herbs, he noticed other things in this tiny space, all that was left to her for growing things. There was a plait of red onions and another of garlic hung up outside, and, set in the shade, he saw a cheese-cloth dripping whey into a bowl.

'Have you got someone you can talk to, Inspector? Really talk?'

He thought of Violetta. Impossible, now.

'My daughter - I can't tell her much about my work, she's too young. But maybe when she's older.'

'You'll be fortunate, then.'

He got up to go.

'Look,' he said, 'It's none of my business. But if I were you, I'd take the offer - if they'll help you move away from here, you should get out. That's what I think, anyway. There's no hope in these places.'

She looked at him, with her deep-set brown eyes tilted upwards in her wrinkled face, and said, '*Eh, bien*, well, you see, Mr. Clever-arsed Policeman, they're the only places I know now.'

He made his way down the graffiti-strewn staircase and then anonymously out and along the walkway where the litter blew around, safely away from Babette's home.

Chapter Fifty-five

Cecile walked into her office and touched the desk almost with surprise at its solidity. This was reality again. She felt almost as if Blenheim and Oxford had been a dream, of strange scenery and architecture that belonged to other worlds.

'They got through straight away,' said her clerk, scratching his head, almost with a puzzled look. 'They still don't know how it was done, apparently, with some sort of a dagger-type weapon that could have been smuggled into the prison. It didn't have to be very long, anyway, just enough to pierce the heart, in the hands of an expert.'

'Bad luck for White Boy,' said Cecile thoughtfully, 'an expert, in the same prison, who must have had some terrible grievance against him.'

'Yes, that's what they said from Cannes.'

'It was Inspector Maubourg?'

'Yes. He wanted to get across the information, and Colas said we could contact you.'

'And call me home.'

'Yes, if you call Versailles home!'

'It's France, anyway.'

They paused for a few moments, staring out at the distant view of the Château, where a long motorcade was whisking some visiting dignitary through the gates. Then Cecile said briskly, 'Well, I'd better get back into harness as soon as possible. What have we got outstanding? The case of the Calvert woman - is it being followed up?'

'Yes, the lake was dragged - no result. Audran's looking at whether there's a connection with the body found near the station. And he's been following up some statement by the Calvert woman's friend, Élise Barrau. Maybe unofficially.'

'That is good work on Audran's part - but it may not get him a commendation.'

'No. Colas doesn't like officers who step out of line, even if they're in the right. We're applying to get an extradition order for Vitek, I take it?'

'Yes. The lab has matched his prints against the marks on the boy's neck - no doubt at all about it. He tried to strangle him, whether for an audience or not.'

'It'll be more difficult to get him convicted of finishing the boy off with the gun.'

'Yes, but he's wanted for rape in England, and attempted murder here, and breaching the immigration laws in both countries. Vitek should be behind bars for a very long time, with all that against him. There's something else, madame, a trivial case in comparison, but one that might have a lot of publicity. The suicide case - old de Vouet.'

'There's nothing to cast any doubt on suicide?'

'No. We have the note, plus evidence from the wife and the doctor that he's been acutely depressed. But the wife - widow, rather, wants to see you. She's preparing a statement to the press, it seems. I told her that was nothing to do with the magistrate's office - we have nothing to do with publicity or journalists.'

'Quite right. But what exactly does she want from me? I'll fit her in, if we can get quarter of an hour in the diary somewhere.'

The woman calling herself the Marquise de Vouet came into Cecile's office that afternoon. She had a rigid bearing, but her eyes were red-rimmed. She began almost as soon as she got in.

'I don't know what one can expect these days, with all sorts of people becoming lawyers and judges ... not the kind of people I am accustomed to deal with.'

Cecile cut her short, feeling simultaneously guilty and irritated.

'Yes, madame, but I am here, you see, and you have to deal with me, so please tell me what you want.'

'My husband, the late Marquis, was driven to his death! Hounded to it!'

'Madame, believe me, I regret that your husband took the course he did. But there are no legal questions over his death: it is quite simply a case of suicide.'

'You insisted on prosecuting him ... you, women like you

especially, are biased against people like us. You hate us, that's the truth. Look at all these cases in the newspapers, all these prominent men persecuted by some miserable little *juge d'instruction*!'

'Please get on with what you have to say to me.'

Cecile avoided using any title: to call the woman madame would have infuriated her, and she could not bear to use the title, 'Marquise' which would stick in her throat.

'Anyone else, some common creature from a tower block, you would have dropped the charges!'

'It is for the Prosecutor to decide whether to press charges or not. I merely investigate the evidence.'

Cecile was uncomfortably aware of a shifting of moral responsibility, even though what she had said was legally perfectly true.

'Yes, but you needn't have pushed things so far. You needn't have investigated the matter at all.'

'I had to do so! Your husband had been accused of theft, and there were several witnesses!'

The woman stood up and was screaming at her now, losing all the control so carefully maintained.

'You're just some little communist tart who wants to pull people like us down! I'll tell the newspapers it's all political - you were persecuting my husband - that you're a left-winger who wanted to bring us down to your level!'

'If you have nothing more to say, please leave my office.'

For a moment, Cecile thought she was going to be attacked, but Jean-Paul had heard the commotion and hastily pushed the door open. Almost spitting with rage, the woman left the office.

Later, a journalist rang up. 'Please tell them,' Cecile said carefully, 'that the Marquis de Vouet, to whom I am extending all respect for the deceased, was innocent of all charges.'

'Innocent? But, *madame le juge* ...'

'Innocent,' she repeated, more firmly. 'The charges were never proved. And he was innocent till proven guilty. So he died an innocent man.'

'It cost me a lot, that admission,' she told Daniel, later.

'But it was right, wasn't it?'

'Yes,' she said wearily. 'It was right. And I didn't understand about the mirror. I mean, why he took it. I think now I do.'

'You seem to get yourself involved in some very odd psychology. About your two Oxford ladies - what do you think really happened?'

'Oh, they had walked a long way, it was hot, they lost their way and wouldn't admit it. They simply got the landscape confused. And then they worked it up in their minds and embellished it with all kinds of details. The truth would have been bound to come out - about Mique's map, for instance. Mique died on the guillotine, by the way. His original map was actually in a library in Modena, not stuffed up a chimney in Montmorency at all. In fact, the Modena archive was known to de Nolhac, the curator at Versailles. He used material from it in one of his books in 1914.'

'Before Moberly and Jourdain mentioned it?'

'Yes. They didn't say anything about the finding of Mique's map up the chimney till the third edition of their book. And that was published in 1924.'

'The year Eleanor Jourdain died?'

'Yes. And the year when Annie Moberly stopped keeping her records.'

Daniel leaned forward and said, 'It was suicide?'

'The doctor said it was a heart attack. That's what it would probably have been anyway. The heart would simply have given out, whether under the strain of some poisonous substance or simply because of stress. They had committed themselves to print, after all - and they were about to be found out on a key point of their story. I think Eleanor Jourdain had been snooping again - perhaps she saw some notes that had an abbreviation of Modena - perhaps she read them upside down, as she had when she researching about the film that had been made in the grounds of Versailles, and assumed 'Mo' or something like it stood for Montmorency. And she didn't know anything about the circumstances, so she made up that fairy-story about the chimney.'

He went to make some coffee. Cecile was still thinking about the past. Moberly and Jourdain, those two ladies from the rigidly genteel background of North Oxford, must have been reading about some very violent and shocking events. Marie-Antoinette had been accused of sexual intrigue with the Princesse de Lamballe, one of her court favourites. After the Revolution when the King and Queen were imprisoned, the Princesse de Lamballe had been required to take an oath forswearing all loyalty to the monarchy. She had refused to do so. A dumpy, foolish, middle-aged woman, she was turned over to the mob, stripped, and guillotined. Her head was stuck on a pole and thrust up before the Queen's windows.

'I suppose she couldn't face the mob,' she said, and found she had spoken aloud, as Daniel came back into the room with the coffee.

'Who, darling?'

'Oh, it doesn't matter now - it's past history,' she said, with relief.

Chapter Fifty-six

Luke kept so silent that they were afraid they'd never break him.

'You don't often feel this in a case,' observed Halley when he talked to Willis on the phone. 'That you're up against someone who really has no feeling at all for human life.'

But Luke had told them in the end, after they had confronted him with Elisaveta. 'That's the one who met us near Oxford. He was telling some of us we could look like students - we could go into the streets there, we wouldn't stand out.'

So Luke had eventually told them what had happened in Versailles.

'Vitek killed the boy?' said Daniel, incredulously, when Cecile told him about it afterwards. 'Just for that? Just as a - a kind of illusion?'

'Yes. It was the canary trick. The boy's life didn't matter, you see. Vitek wanted to create an illusion, that Marina was crazy - that way, no one would take any notice of what she said. "This woman runs round historic buildings imagining fantasies! She's obsessed with the past, look at those mad old ladies she's studying, it's all preyed on her mind!" That's what everyone would think. And, hey presto, the 'body' vanishes.'

'That's really evil.'

'The whole thing has a particular ring of malice to it, a personal touch, you might say. That's why I think it was Luke's idea, originally. Because it would have affected Marina's career - no-one would have taken her research seriously. She'd been reading about those Victorian women and it affected her mind: that's the interpretation everyone would have put upon it. She had fantasies at Blenheim and again at Versailles. It would certainly have meant an end to her academic life. And of course, when we looked for a reason for such a murder - it seemed non-existent.'

'It's hard to believe anyone would be so ruthless as to commit murder simply because he was staging a scene,' commented Daniel.

'Why he didn't just set up a charade - have the boy play a part? Why was it necessary to actually kill him?'

'Because he didn't want to make the same mistake twice. He'd almost let the girl at Woodstock get out of his clutches - there was to be no opportunity for the boy to escape, and perhaps for the truth to come out. I don't think Luke expected him to kill the boy - he just suggested the charade. He was probably terrified himself when he learned just how callous Vitek is.'

'To kill someone - just for that?'

Cecile answered slowly, 'I don't think those people he smuggles through Europe mean anything to him - no more than the canaries do to the conjuror.'

'But didn't Marina say they were in eighteenth-century dress?' It was characteristic of Daniel to want to get all the details pinned into place.

'It's very easy to suggest something like that, especially if you're in appropriate surroundings, with the right backdrop of a famous old building, and somebody who's probably walked through it looking at portraits of characters in frills and silk. All you need for a man really is perhaps a loose, ruffled shirt, tight trousers, maybe to buy a wig from a costumier. That was the boy's bad luck, I think. Lieutenant Audran said he had long hair - in fact, he took the victim for a girl, at first. So maybe that's why he was chosen.'

'Just because he wore his hair long?'

'He had long, fair hair, didn't he? It could just have been tied back in a ponytail, the way some young men wear it nowadays - the effect at a distance could have passed as one of those eighteenth-century perruques worn at court, especially if some talcum powder was brushed into it. It would have meant one less problem, and afterwards, one less thing to dispose of. According to Luke Elmer, they rehearsed it with the boy - all but the final scene of course. Vitek knew of Marina's movements through Elmer - it wasn't difficult, I expect, to follow her from the hotel, just like any other tourists. Then they walked on ahead, and Vitek and the boy, dressed up just a little, rushed out of the temple where they were hiding, and enacted an alarming scene - seemingly, a murder.'

'Why a murder - why not just something like the business at Blenheim, where the girl was seen running away and being caught. Why go so far as to stage a murder?'

'Because it was essential that Marina should make a fuss,' answered Cecile. 'She had to cause a scene, call the police. She had to have seen a terrible event, not just perhaps a lovers' quarrel or something of the sort. The whole point was to bring her sanity seriously into doubt. And murder is the most serious thing any human being can claim to witness. The boy will have thought it was all some sort of a joke, a charade, I don't doubt.'

'Then they discarded their props, as it were -'

'And when they got safely away from the scene, he did it in earnest. To make sure the little bird never sang.'

Chapter Fifty-seven

'Louis?'

'Where are you phoning from, Cecile? Are you still in England?'

'No, I'm back in Versailles. I'd like to speak to Flo, please.'

'Yes, but listen I'm not having my child placed in danger. Let's get that clear - if you want to take risks, that's up to you, but I don't want Florence there!'

'Louis, it's settled. The man is dead, I mean, the man who was threatening me. Maubourg's been talking to the police here. They're satisfied there's no problem any more. You don't have any justification for keeping Flo there.'

'This is the best place for her, you know that, Cecile. Babette wanted me to send her to Marseilles - well, I told her what I thought of that! I'm not having my daughter brought up in a tower block in Marseilles, where half of them don't even speak French and the rest can barely write it!'

Cecile told herself not to be goaded by Louis. She knew his tricks of old: he was a clever lawyer, skilled at rousing the hackles of opponents whom he wanted to show in a bad light. She had learned that painfully, during their marriage and afterwards. He would have made an excellent court-room advocate, but he had preferred to devote himself to property law - fewer pyrotechnics, but the fees came in much more steadily. She said aloud, 'Louis, let me talk to her, please. Let me speak to my daughter.'

There was a pause and then Florence's voice came on the line, small but clear.

'*Maman*?'

'Darling, listen, tell me, did you want to go to *grand-mère* in Marseilles?'

Florence didn't say anything, and Cecile added, 'You can tell me exactly how you feel about it. Don't worry, darling. Where would you like to be?'

There was the sound of a small, choked exclamation.

'She's trying to be brave,' thought Cecile. 'Damn it, what sort of a life do I lead, where my child has to pretend to me?'

Florence said, 'I want to be with you, Maman. That's all.'

Chapter Fifty-eight

The whole Land Rover had a pungent odour of horse, which must have been secondary, deriving from the harnesses thrown into the back. There were complicated webs and straps of damp-looking leather with rings and buckles, a heap of tackle thrown over a shabby box with a peeling blue cross painted on it. Or perhaps the horsey whiff emanated from Julien himself, whose bow legs fitted uncomfortably into the driver's seat, and whose hands gripped the steering wheel relentlessly, as if he were determined to master a strange beast.

They bucked off along the paths, Audran doing up his seat-belt as a gesture of protective optimism. He could tell more or less where they were: not far beyond the grounds of the Château, but in grounds that seemed almost like open country. They were moving through unremarkable scenery, clumps of tall trees, past long fences, Julien peering out through his window at intervals and jabbing a finger at the landscape.

'Good going here - we take 'em out in all weathers.'

'Go more slowly - go at the same sort of speed you would, if you were riding.'

They slowed down to what seemed like a snail's speed to Audran. 'How fast we move now!' he thought. 'Strange, what had it been like, when this was the fastest anyone could go? a bit faster maybe, if you were galloping on a really good racehorse, but not much. No wonder we talk about the "pace of modern life".'

Aloud, he said, 'How far is it to the place? Where you noticed the horse behaving strangely?'

'Well, I'd hardly say it was even strangely,' said Julien. 'He just flickered his ears a bit.'

'Whatever it was - as if he heard something, you said?'

'Quite close. In those beeches over there, I'd say.'

Audran saw a glimpse of something through the tree-trunks, a red-brick wall and a grey slate roof.

'Can you turn off the path? I want to take a look.'

They turned off the main track, but it narrowed to a point where the Land Rover was bouncing along grass verges, and Audran thought only a smaller vehicle could have got through. Julien brought the vehicle to a halt and Audran got out. He slammed the door behind him. Julien looked after him passively as he walked towards the entrance.

It was an isolated building, a lodge-keeper's cottage, he would have guessed, that might once have been part of the royal estate, a couple of centuries ago, maybe. The brickwork was a soft orange-red, crumbling and velvety with age, and the chimneystack looked as if it had slipped sideways, somehow.

Moving round the building, he saw an outhouse with a stone sink and a pump. The floor was wet. Lifting the handle of the pump, it moved stiffly under his hand, and as he pushed it down again, a trickle of rusty water ran into the sink. There was a stinking smell coming from a stall beyond the pump, a smell which he identified without difficulty. Recent.

And beneath that familiar stench a trace of something else, something more elemental still, far beyond the odour of farmyard privy, which was almost comforting in comparison.

The tall windows, with arched ornamental panes at the top, had grimy rippled old glass through which he could see a wavering interior. There was only one room downstairs, an expanse of old floor-boards stretching away to a staircase. There was a long object in the room: he wiped the glass with his hand and made out a couch, worn and sagging. But a modern thing, covered in some sort of cheap flowered material. And it stood in a space of floor that was tracked with mud.

He knocked at the door, and the banging sounded horribly loud in the wilderness: suddenly, he remembered children's story-books, tales of Hansel and Gretel and the little children who had got lost in the wood, pictures of old crones and twisted chimney-stacks.

He called out a couple of times, and listened.

Nothing.

He went back to the Land Rover. Julien leaned across and opened the passenger door.

Audran stood with his hand on the door.

He had no warrant to get in to the premises, no reason to make a forced entry.

The door was flimsy, though.

It was the merest ghost of a chance, scarcely worth following up at all, let alone making an illegal break-in without a magistrate's warrant.

'What you want to do?'

Julien's bronzed face peered at him.

Audran didn't reply.

'I do have sufficient evidence,' he told himself. 'Enough for suspicion. Enough to allow me to make an entry.'

He could already hear a lawyer starting on this one.

'And tell me, Inspector Audran, you broke into these premises because a horse - a very sagacious animal, but even so, let us admit it, a dumb brute - a horse had pricked up its ears? You converse with the animals, Inspector? No doubt we will have police dogs giving their testimony in the near future!'

'There was the smell.'

Hopeless justification. It would sound utterly ludicrous. A horse's ears and a bad smell.

The end of his brief career could be in sight. 'But all the same,' he said to himself stubbornly, 'there was the working pump. That looked as if someone had drawn water recently.'

'Perhaps to water one of the aforesaid equine witnesses?'

No, that wouldn't do in court, either.

He went to the Land Rover and said, 'I've got to make a call.'

Audran was so preoccupied with worrying about the bureaucratic legalities he had to comply with that he didn't look in the end stall of the stable building. So he didn't see the shiny Yamaha bike leaning against the partition, the heat still rising from its engine.

Chapter Fifty-nine

Cecile's voice came down the line, tinny under the roof of the vehicle. Damn, thought Audran, maybe he should have chosen a better place... But he could hear her, anyway.

'Yes, I'll give you a *commission rogatoire*. On that evidence.'

'You will?'

She was laying herself on the line, they both knew it, in spite of the power of the *juge d'instruction* to order entry and questioning.

'I'll have to go back to the station and wait till it gets there.'

'No. This is an emergency. I give you verbal authority now - and I'll issue written authorisation to back it up.'

He went back to the door, banged again, and when there was no answer, took a deep breath, looked back at the Land Rover, couldn't see Julien, hoped there was no witness, and took a kick at the lock.

It didn't give, and he realised that it was much stronger than he had thought. But this in itself gave him a new determination. He bent down and peered at it more closely.

This shouldn't be a strong modern lock, it should be a rusting old thing, to go with the cottage itself.

He went round to a window and repeated the kicking process. The old frame gave way without too much difficulty. 'Wet-rot,' said Audran to himself. 'He didn't get that fixed.'

There was a crunching sound as he knocked glass out of the frame, and old flakes of dried paint and putty flew through the air.

He advanced over the old timbers, his feet echoing.

Up the shambling steps that had once constituted a staircase, with an unexpectedly graceful sweeping handrail, calling out as he went. 'Anyone there?'

There was one long bare room under the roof, nothing else. The dormer windows seemed to be up among the tree-tops.

Downstairs, he rapped one foot on the floor and listened. There did seem to be a hollowness.

The trap door was at the back of the staircase. He pulled it up without much trouble, and the stench told him what was there. Human, rotting, rich and stinking, like the outhouse.

Élise was right, he thought. This is the place. But he wouldn't ever tell her what it was like.

He peered down, and realised he needed his torch, and, fumbling about in his jacket pocket, produced it. The stairs were really decaying here, and he held on to a hand rail that seemed equally likely to pitch him down headlong.

The floor was covered in scraps and bits of rag and there was a puddle of something sticky beside an old mattress. He shone the torch along the top of the mattress, and it looked filthy, but bare. But then he saw there was another, underneath, and pulled the top one aside.

At first he thought she was dead. She was almost stifled. Her thin body had fallen into a hollow in the lower mattress, and the second one had nearly covered her face. Somehow, she had managed to turn her head sideways, instead of having her mouth pressed into the filthy old flock above her, and a little air must have got to her through the gap. She looked like a mummy, her face shrunken and stained, her body dehydrated.

He was lifting her head, trying to check for signs of life, getting out his mobile with his other hand, when he heard a creaking sound above.

'Julien?'

No response.

He called again, and, like a soughing of the wind in the trees, came a gust of air and with it a shape that launched itself at him down the stairs and straight on to his back. His torch rolled away. He felt a blow at the back of his head, and, outlined against the faint daylight that came from the trap, saw a head peering at him, and an arm raising something aloft into the darkness, something long and heavy, that came crashing down just as he managed to roll away. But then he saw that the figure had produced something else, that there was a gun, as well, and knew that there was virtually no chance now.

The shot sounded unbelievably loud in the confined space. It seemed to ricochet around the cellar, at the same time as a long, resounding, high-pitched scream. Audran was dazed by the noise, but managed to take in one thing.

The shot had been fired from above, from the trap-door.

Groping for his torch, reaching for the beam of light, he at last shone it upwards. Julien was descending the steps, waving something heavy in his hand.

'Christ, what a stink! It's a pistol - it's all right - I'm licensed to carry it. For shooting horses on the spot - in case we get a serious injury, broken leg or something. Hate to do it, but we don't want to wait for a vet.'

'How did you ...?'

'I saw a bloke sneaking round the side of the house - didn't like the way he was carrying something nasty-looking. I think it was an old starting-handle. Then I looked down here and saw him pulling a gun on you. God Almighty - is that a woman?'

'Yes - and she's alive.'

Chapter Sixty

They were rolling through the mountains behind the Provençal coast line, and Cecile felt that she was opening up like some tropical plant in the heat.

'I was brought up in this climate,' she said to Daniel. 'It's what suits me, really. Doesn't matter if it's in a city, or in beautiful countryside like this.'

The red and purple landscape of the Esterel range was ahead of them, its strange futuristic rocks fractured in the landscape like a cubist painting. Between the mountains ran a green river valley, the turquoise water reflecting the cloudless sky.

'Soon be there, darling.'

'How did you know I wanted to set off right away?'

Daniel didn't answer, and she thought, 'He just did. That's why I love him.'

They turned off the road and bounced up a track.

There, at the top, was the solid Provençal farmhouse, the mas of Louis' parents. And of his grandparents, and all of his forefathers, the foundation of their wealth and solid bourgeois prosperity.

In spite of the phone call, Cecile was nervous. Suppose Flo didn't want them, after all, didn't need them? Suppose she was really happier with Louis' parents? They were her own grandparents, after all, blood must count for something.

Amélie was standing outside the door of the farmhouse, shielding her eyes with her hand. She turned as the car approached, seemingly calling through the doorway to someone inside.

'I must try and build some bridges with her,' Cecile said to Daniel.

'You don't have to, you know. She was pretty dreadful to you.'

Yes, she had accused Cecile of terrible things. 'You just want to sacrifice your child to your career,' she had shouted at her, one day. 'Poor little soul - she might as well not have a mother!'

But maybe the time had come to try and bury the past.

Otherwise, if Cecile wanted to reclaim her daughter, it might soon be too late.

They were close to the farmhouse now, and Cecile saw a tiny figure rushing out of the door.

'There she is.'

Amélie was hurrying after the child, but Cecile called to Daniel, 'Stop the car! Please!' and as he braked to a halt, she leapt out and ran as fast as she could along the path, not caring about the stones and thorns, and now the child was running towards her, and the sturdy little body flung itself into Cecile's arms.

'Maman! Oh, Maman!'

Cecile dashed the back of her hand across her face and felt the wetness of her tears.

'Ridiculous,' she thought. 'We're both weeping.'

Aloud, she only said, 'Oh, Flo! Oh, darling Flo!'

'I'm Florence now,' said the child, proudly.

Author's Note

In telling the story of Charlotte Anne Moberly and Eleanor Jourdain, the respected Oxford ladies who claimed to have seen ghosts in the gardens of Versailles, I have been as historically accurate as possible. Their book, *An Adventure*, was first published in 1911. Another edition in 1913 contained plans of the grounds and the 1924 edition contained the story about the map found up the chimney. The quotations on pages 159 and 162 are taken from the 1911 edition.

Readers who want to pursue the history of these strange events may also want to read Lucille Iremonger's book, *The Ghosts of Versailles, Miss Moberly, Miss Jourdain and their Adventures*, which was published in 1957. Eleanor Jourdain's sister, Melicent, wrote a poetic little book, *A Childhood*, under the name of Joan Arden.

I would like to thank the staff of the Bodleian Library, Oxford: unfailingly helpful and displaying at all times what Hemingway declared to be the characteristic of heroism, 'grace under pressure'.